Moon,
Have You Met
My Mother?

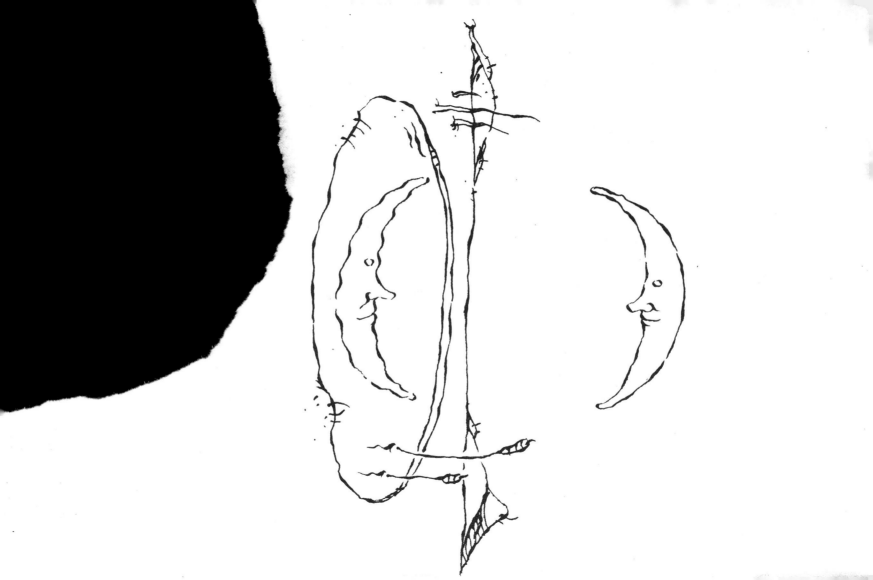

Moon, Have You Met My Mother?

The collected poems of Karla Kuskin

Illustrations by Sergio Ruzzier

LAURA GERINGER BOOKS
An Imprint of HarperCollinsPublishers

Moon, Have You Met My Mother?

Copyright © 2003 by Karla Kuskin

For information address HarperCollins Children's Books, a division of HarperCollins Publishers, 1350 Avenue of the Americas, New York, NY 10019.

www.harperchildrens.com

Library of Congress Cataloging-in-Publication Data

Kuskin, Karla.

Moon, have you met my mother? : The collected poems of Karla Kuskin / illustrations by Sergio Ruzzier.

p.   cm.

ISBN 0-06-027173-6 — ISBN 0-06-027174-4 (lib. bdg)

1. Children's poetry, American. [1. American poetry.] 1. Title.

PS3561.U79 M66 2003

811'.54—dc21

2001024620

CIP

AC

Typography by Alicia Mikles

1 2 3 4 5 6 7 8 9 10

❖

First Edition

Be well, Bill Bell,

with love from me

—KSKB

Contents

Introduction   ix

I Do Not Understand Arf   1

I Do Not Wish I Were a Cat   9

Pigeons Is a Pretty Word   33

Buggity, Buggity, Bug   53

A Wizard Had a Lizard   71

Bears Don't Purrr, They Grrrrr   91

Spring Again, Spring Again, Spring . . .   109

Five, Four, Three, Too Hot!   123

Good-bye Toes   147

Ice Is Nice   159

I Will Not Eat Beets   191

I Need to Read   219

There Is a Me Inside of Me   235

Isn't It Queer Than an Ear Can Hear?   267

Moon, Have You Met My Mother?   289

Acknowledgments   313

Index   319

Introduction

ONCE, SIXTY YEARS AGO, there was a child

who had some storms inside herself

but was, on the surface, rather mild.

She had a round face,

dark eyes and hair,

and she spent a lot of time

drawing pictures and

writing words

that came out of the storms

or the mildness

or from some other mysterious where.

Prose she wrote, and, at other times, rhyme

over days, months, and many years.

Words, words, uncounted words

that rubbed together

with small explosions;

popping, snapping, splattering,

dancing, jangling, shattering.

Words that made her laugh and think,

or feel, at times, quite full of tears.

And she drew pictures to go with the words,

that was something she loved to do.

As a girl she went to school

but then, of course, she grew

and began making books

out of the words that she wrote

and the drawings that she drew.

Days, months, many years went by.

The woman, who had been a child,

had children of her own.

They ran around playing and dancing

and laughing and scrapping.

They read a lot of books, including hers,

and wrote and drew and also grew.

After they finished school

they went to work too,

clicking camera shutters and printing

photographic prints

in blacks and whites

and different colored tints.

Her grown children had children of their own

who were her grandchildren.

So she wrote new books,

more than a few,

for them and for their friends.

And all of them read and looked at the world together

while taking long walks in many places in every weather

and drawing drawings without end.

But when her grown children

and their children went home late in the day,

she would sit in an old chair

looking at pictures of her old life

and read words she had written, some old, some new.

Then feeling quite old and grey

she would write a little more

the way she always did

when she had thoughts

to put into words

that she felt she wanted to say.

And the words she wrote,

sometimes she wondered why,

sometimes she wondered how,

are an introduction to all these words

that fill the poems

that fill this book

that you are reading now.

Karla Kuskin

I Do Not
Understand Arf

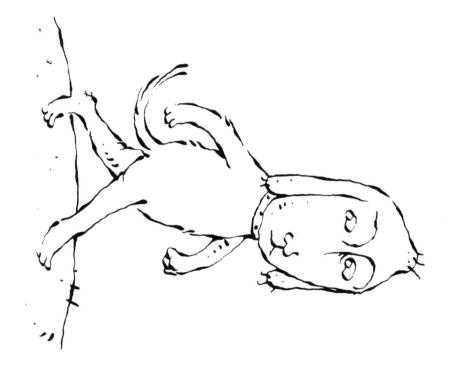

I do not understand

ARF

how people

ARF

GROWL

BARK

can walk around on two

ARF

legs.

I see them in the park

BARK

and all around the town.

They walk around on just two legs

without

BARK

falling down.

ARF.

You are the kind of dog I love

because

you are a walking hill of hair.

And even though I cannot see your

eyes

ears

nose

or paws,

I somehow know

that you

are under there.

I would like to have a pet
any kind at all.
Something big,
something small,
something sleeping in the hall
would be just fine.
I would like to have a pet.
Will you be mine?

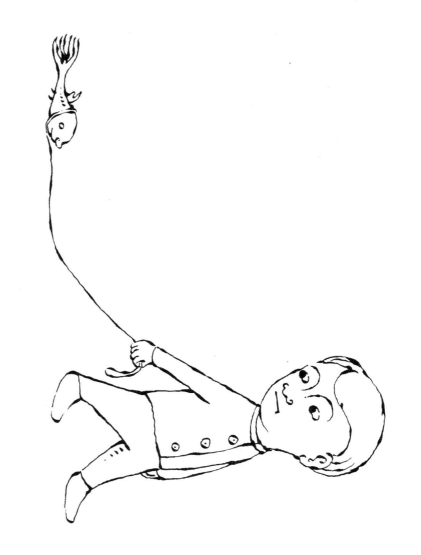

I have a little guppy.
I would rather have a puppy.

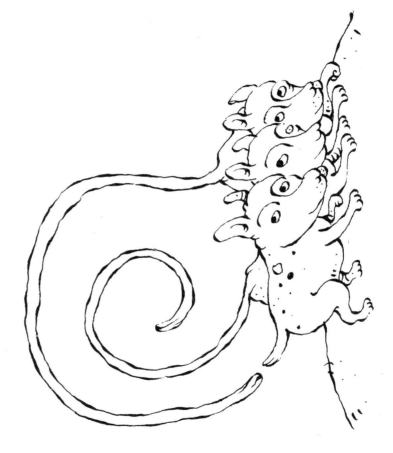

T he running dogs begin to bark
in the morning early.
Their ears blow back,
their tails are flags,
long and short and curly.

I Do Not Wish
I Were a Cat

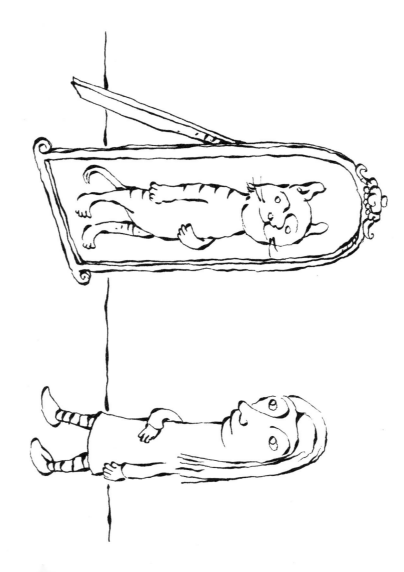

I do not wish I were a cat
with fine black whiskers
smoky fur.
I do not want a tail and paws
I only wish that I could purr.

When a cat is asleep
there is nothing asleep
that is quite so asleep
as a cat.

She has finished with darting,
careening and leaping
now even the soft air around her is sleeping.

This cat
walks into the room and across the floor,
under a chair, around the bed,
behind the table and out the door.

I'm sitting on the chair
and I don't see where he is.
I don't see one hair of his.
I just hear the floorboards scarcely squeak.
This cat comes and goes
on invisible toes.
The sneak.

Examining the breeze.
A package neatly wrapped with tail
flicks a whisker
pleased.

Upon the stair.
Taking the air.
Unquestioned owner
of the comfortable chair.

Napping everywhere
stretched in the sun
as if the sun were hers
awash in warmth
and furs.

The flow of a cat walking
over the lawn
to place herself like a soft stone
in the middle of the paper
I am working on.

The terrible cat of black velvet fur

will leap at your legs

with a thunderous purrr

flash through the air

to a lap

or a chair

nibble your dinner

and probably stare

at your face and your frown

as she daintily tears

the chop you were eating

and swallows it down.

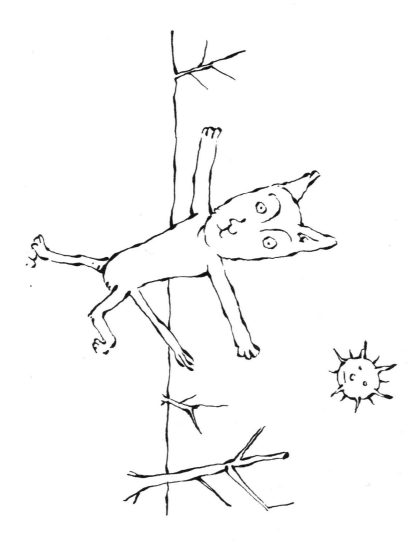

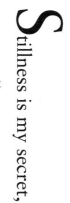

Stillness is my secret,
secret stillness.
Sitting in a stream of winter sun,
sunning on the window radiator.
I'm a cat.
I don't need anyone.

Amanda was an alley cat.

Not fluffy,

she was dusty, scarred and lean.

She lived,

like other alley cats,

behind old walls,

beneath parked cars.

She did not know that grass was green.

She did not know the night had stars,

just streetlights

taxicabs

more cars

to hide beneath

to dodge between.

She hunted rats.

She ran from man.

And loved

(as much as she loved anything at all)

a garbage can.

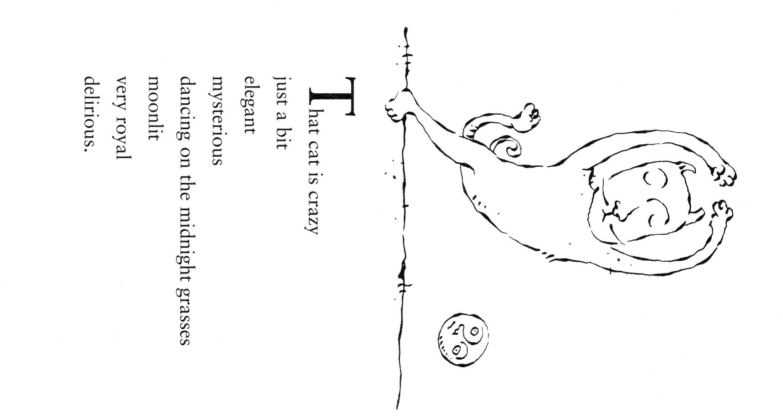

That cat is crazy
just a bit
elegant
mysterious
dancing on the midnight grasses
moonlit
very royal
delirious.

Cats take naps

from dawn to dawn.

They nap on anything they're on,

a pillow

antique chair

or lawn.

And when their need to nap is gone,

they stretch

and yawn

and look around for something else

it might be nice

to nap upon.

In August once
just Charlie and the cat
driving to the island in a small white car.
And then
when they were neither here nor there,
stopping for gas
along the road in Maine,
Charlie looked in to check the cat
pat the back
scratch an ear
and looked again.

In August

going down a country road .

at sixty per

our much loved cat, dear Ace,

jumped out the window,

left hand rear,

confused perhaps

or simply filled with fear

of driving.

Charlie searched and searched for her

but she was gone for good.

He walked the rutted, wooded roads

calling her name,

miles back

and years ago

in August. Once.

We've had some other cats since then.

They haven't been the same.

I

f you,
like me,
were made of fur
and the sun warmed you,
like me,
you'd purr.

Ears back

tail low

toe

by toe

by toe

our Tootsie creeps

looking for a little trouble

while the city sleeps.

Julia loves her Rosalie.

Rosalie the cat.

Julia pets her nosealie.

Soft, disdainful Rosalie.

Steps upon her toesalie

pulls her tail and

ohsalie,

Julia has a scratch.

While Rosalie guileless

and practically smileless

suns quietly, sly on her mat.

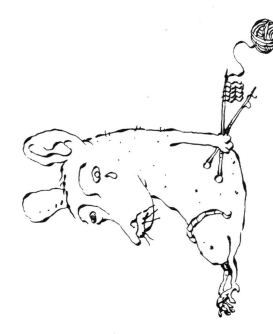

There was a mouse
who used to sit
about the house
all day and knit
until the cat
got wind of it.

The cat
and all her little kittens
came and ate
that mouse's mittens.

I had a cat,
grey
soft
fat

given to grrring
quite softly
and prrrring.
Slipped off one morning
near the green glen.
That was my cat
who was not seen again.

I had a dog,
noisy and yellow
very cold nose
wonderful fellow.

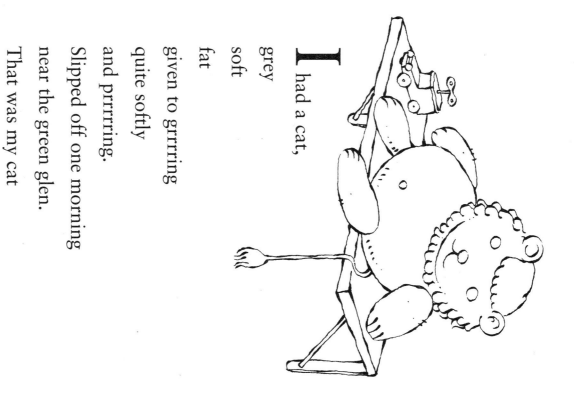

Trotted one evening
out after a pack
of dog-footed friends
and never came back.

I had a bird,
bright blue in a cage
sang without cease
on his miniature stage.
Sat on my shoulder
looked in my eye
sailed out the window
and into the sky.

I have a lion,
furry and kind
sits on a shelf
near the autos that wind.
Eyes wild and golden
tail like a tuft
he never will slip out and leave me.
He's stuffed.

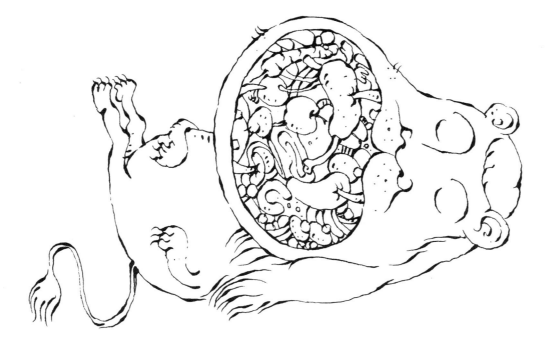

The lion looks extremely proud.
But when he eats,
he chews too loud.

One thing that you can say about roaring.

It is not boring.

And if rushing around the jungle being king

is your kind of thing

you might find the life of a lion

worth tryin'.

The night is black
and so am I.
Black and strong I wait
and lie along the branch
to spring and eat
some soft weak thing
walking the night black path along
beneath my feet.
The night is still
and so am I.
Lying in wait
I spring.
A cry.
I have my feast.
The jungle knows the jaguar
and trembles at the beast.

Take a word like cat

and build around it;

a fur room over here

a long meow

floating from the chimney like a smoke tail.

Draw with words.

Balance them like blocks.

Carve word furniture:

a jar of pussy willows,

catkins, phlox,

milk in a dish,

catnip pillows,

a silver bell,

a plaster bird,

an eaten fish.

When everything is perfect in its place

step back to view the home

that you have built of words around your word.

It is a poem.

Pigeons Is a Pretty Word

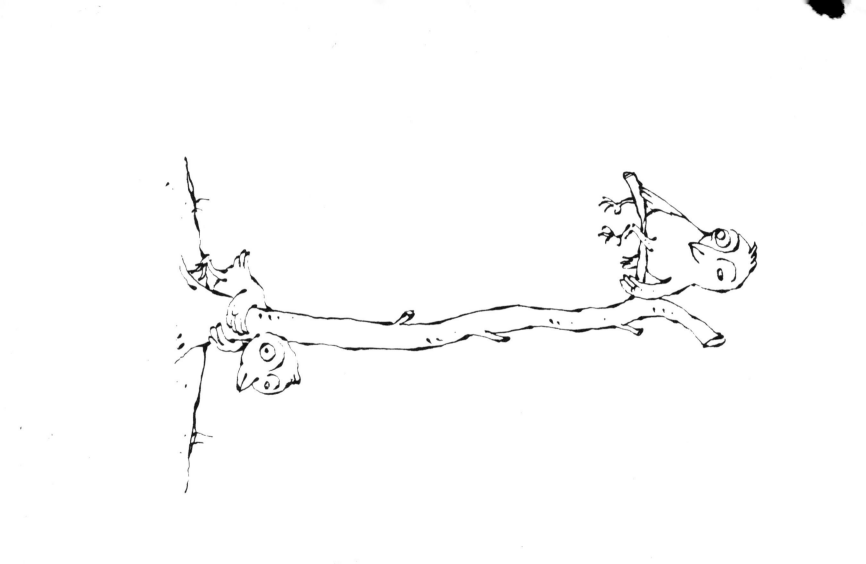

Pigeons is a pretty word.

Pigeons.

Pigeons are a funny bird.

Pigeons.

Toeing out with silly care

shaped a little like a pear

inclined to cock small heads

and stare

at where?

Nowhere.

Pigeons.

Pigeons do not skim the sky.

It seems they'd rather hop than fly

though no one knows exactly why.

Pigeons.

Pigeons love a dusty crumb.

The fact is that

they're pretty dumb.

Pigeons.

M

My bird is small.
My bird is shy.
It does not sing.
It cannot fly.
It does no tricks
and that is fine.

I love my bird.
My bird is mine.

One jay

two jay

kitty got a blue jay.

Three jay

four jay

there isn't any more jay.

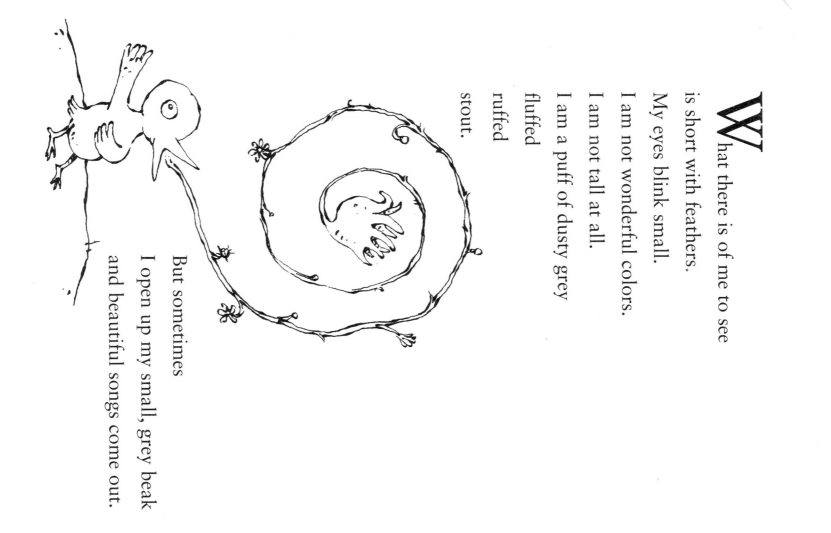

What there is of me to see
is short with feathers.
My eyes blink small.
I am not wonderful colors.
I am not tall at all.
I am a puff of dusty grey
fluffed
ruffed
stout.

But sometimes
I open up my small, grey beak
and beautiful songs come out.

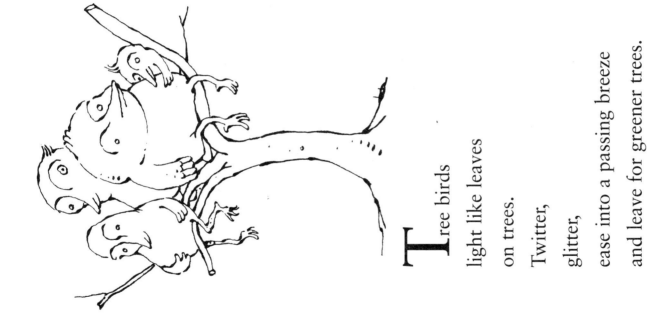

Tree birds
light like leaves
on trees.
Twitter,
glitter,
ease into a passing breeze
and leave for greener trees.

One raven

black

from front

excepting beak

to back,

blue black, contemplates,

and boasts aloud

that he owns everything around:

Earth, corn, sand.

Boy

is he proud.

The sun is his,

the barley there,

that tree,

that rock and what is on it:

me.

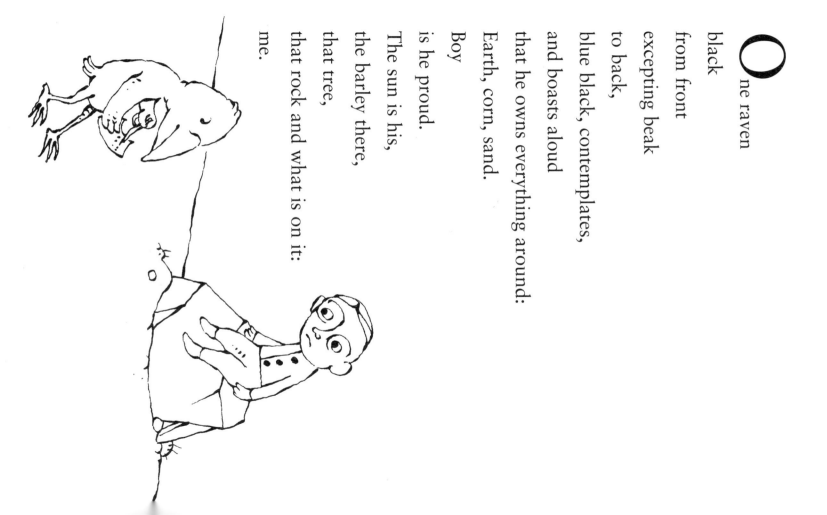

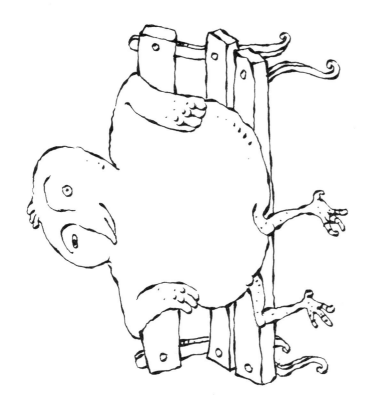

Blue bird on a branch.

Big bird on a twig.

Red bird on a ranch.

Wild bird on a wig.

Broad bird on a bench.

Bored bird on a pig.

Third bird in a bunch.

Blurred bird does a jig.

"Bird

May I borrow your feathers?
May I rest on the air
gliding as you do?
Let me be a bird too."

"Cat
keep away.
I'm a bird
feathered, frail, flying free.
But if I may borrow your tail
I'll try lying in sun pools.
I'll borrow your whiskers and purr.
I'll be feathered, frail, flying
and furred.
My self and my enemy
one
cat-bird."

My home is a white dome

under me.

It is very quiet.

My home is a bright dome

over me.

It is very quiet.

I rest

in my domed home

in the middle of a small sea.

Me.

I am very quiet

sleeping.

The dome cracks.

The sea leaves.

I wake

cheeping.

If I were a bird,
I would chirp like a bird
with a high little cry.
I would not say a word.
I would sit in my nest
with my head on my chest,
being a bird.

If I were a fish,
I would swim like a fish
silently finning
with nary a swish,
just finning through seaweed
to search for a free weed,
being a fish.

If I were a larkspur,
I'd stand in the sun,
growing up slowly
until I was done.

I'd rest in the breeze
with some leaves on my knees,
being a larkspur.

If I were a sandwich,
I'd sit on a plate
and think of my middle
until someone ate

me.
End of the sandwich.

There is a fence
around our house.
There is a catbird
on the fence.
The catbird will not tie his shoes.
If birds wore shoes
this might make sense.

Leander, Leander,
I will not meander
out after a gander with you.
The rills are too rilly,
the hills are too hilly,
the sky is too sparkling blue.
The sun is too low
and the moon is too high,
the dewdrops are dripping,
there's flounder to fry.
There's bacon and cake
and a number of slices
of Limburger cheese,
and there also are ices.
Meander, Leander,
I say it with candor,
return here whenever you wish
and we will eat gander
upon the veranda
out of a light lavender dish . . . .
with fish.

I am proud.

My head is as green as an apple

and my voice is loud.

When I talk

it comes out in a marvelous squawk.

Everybody jumps.

I crack sweet nuts

and sit

spitting shells and splitting pits.

When that gets dull

I tear paper into little bits.

Then I split and spit some more

and watch them rush to sweep the floor.

At night

all the funny people come to dinner

dressed in jewels that clank and shiny leathers

to hide the fact that they do not have feathers.

They gabble, rattle, chitter, chatter
in mouse high squeaks
and low bear growls,
speaking about something called "war"
and someplace called "Downtown"
and someone called "Mrs."
and what she wore the afternoon they met her.
People's talk sounds boring.
Parrot's talk sounds better.

Squawk.

Do you hear the parrot squawk?
He's talking to
a celery stalk.
The parrot likes to squawk and shout
and throw a lot of seeds about.

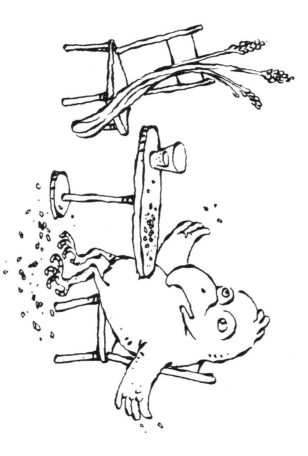

The gulls are not as far as I from you.

The crows are not as far from you as I.

The sky

the disappearing sky

is not as distant on this day

it's true

as I

within my mind

am far from you.

Buggity, Buggity, Bug

Buggity
buggity
bug
wandering aimlessly
buggishly smug
when all of a sudden along came a shoe
out with another shoe
wandering too.
The shoes went on wandering:
left,
right,
left,
splat.

Bugs
very frequently perish like that.

A bug sat in a silver flower
thinking silver thoughts.
A bigger bug out for a walk
climbed up that silver flower stalk
and snapped the small bug down his jaws
without a pause
without a care
for all the bug's small silver thoughts.
It isn't right
it isn't fair
that big bug ate that little bug
because that little bug was there.

He also ate his underwear.

I t makes me squirm
to watch a worm.

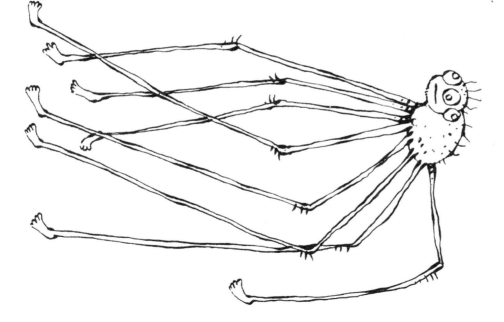

Spiders are all right, I guess,
or would be
if their legs were less.

I am watering the plants.

I'm also watering the ants.

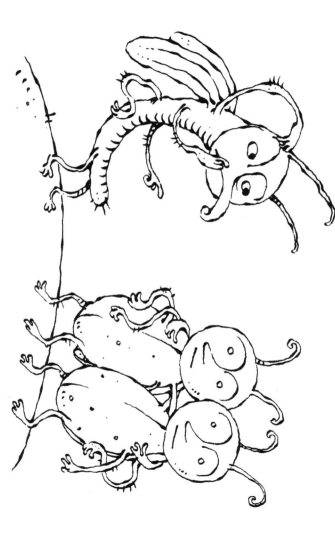

M any people who are smart
in physics, French and math and art
cannot tell two bugs apart.

Bugs are just not very smart
in math or physics, French or art.
But *they* can tell two bugs apart.

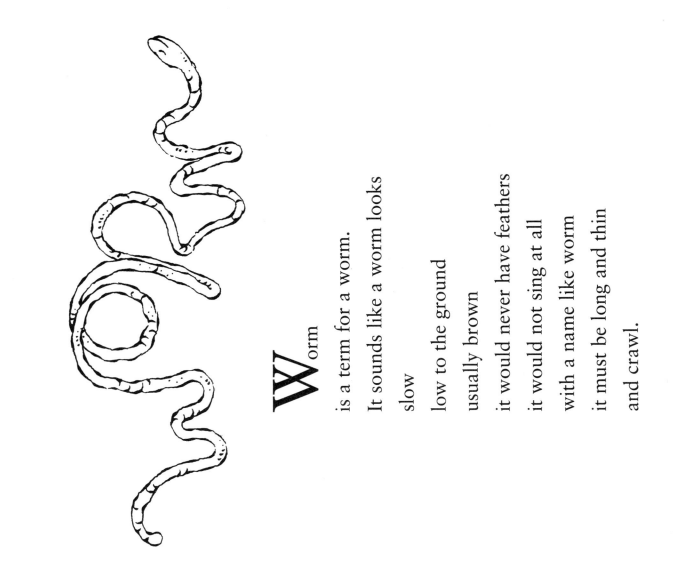

Worm

is a term for a worm.

It sounds like a worm looks

slow

low to the ground

usually brown

it would never have feathers

it would not sing at all

with a name like worm

it must be long and thin

and crawl.

All my legs were very tired.
I had walked, I think, forever
when I came upon a mountain
wide and high as any mountain
standing quite alone.
"That's no mountain,"
said my mother.
"That is just a stone."

We walked on
me and my mother
past a dragon that was not
a dragon
but a caterpillar.
Past a very little pot
with some water in the bottom.
"Look," I said, "a lake."
"You are small," my mother told me.
"And you make a small mistake."

All my feet were very weary

I looked up to see the sky

and I saw a tree above me

tall and leafy

green and high.

"That's no tree," my mother told me.

"That is just a plant.

It is leafy green and little.

It looks tall

because you're smaller

than most things are,"

said my mother.

Mother is an ant.

B ugs never speak.
I wonder why?
Perhaps they're shy.

I walk,
birds fly,
caterpillars pill.

You'd think they would get tired
pilling up a hill.

You'd think they'd find it boring
pilling across a plain.

If I were a caterpillar
and had somewhere really far to go
I would pill on over to Grand Central Station
and take a train.

I am very fond of bugs.
I kiss them
and I give them hugs.

When the blossoms blossom

and the new leaves dance

something small begins to crawl.

The question is what is it?

The answer is it's ants.

Bug
met a dragon
in the park.

La la.

The moon was down

the night was dark.

La la.

The dragon opened his mouth

and fearful flames frothed north by south

and west by east.

The bug deceased.

La la.

A Wizard
Had a Lizard

A wizard
had a lizard.
They really were a team.
The wizard
loved the lizard.
The lizard loved ice cream.

Let me tell you all about me.
Children love me,
you're a child.
All my heads are green and handsome.
All my eyes are red and wild.
All my toes have claws upon them.
All the claws have hooks.
I blow smoke through all my noses.
It is hotter than it looks.
All my tails have points upon them.
All my teeth are sharp and blue.
I won't bite you very badly.
I am fond of you.
All my scales are shaped like arrows.
They will hurt you if you touch.
So, although I know you'll love me,
do not pet me very much.

Look,

here comes an awful dragon.

Wait,

I think his tail is wagging.

What's the good of a wagon
without any dragon
to pull you for mile after mile?
An elegant lean one
a gold-tinted green one
wearing a dragonly smile.
You'll sweep down the valleys
you'll sail up the hills
your dragon will shine in the sun
and as you rush by
the people will cry
"I wish that my wagon had one!"

Smoke comes out of the dragon's nose.

Claws come out of

the dragon's toes.

Flames

flame from the dragon's mouth,

east and west

and north and south.

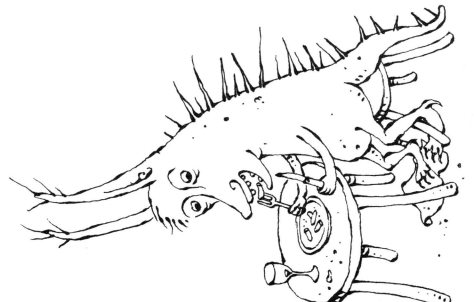

The dragon walks
for miles and miles.
He eats up people.
Then he smiles.
The dragon smiles
because he knows
that nothing tastes as good
as toes.

Come picture this lovely and frightening scene;
you're in the river just floating.
You're green.
The sun is so warm on your back
that you smile
and boats filled with people
speed off for a mile
at the terrible sight
of your teeth sharp as knives.
Birds vanish like arrows
and call for their wives.
You turn with the breezes
and flick your broad tail
and thousands of fishes
writhe, quiver and quail.

So if you're a swimmer
who's fond of a dish
of low flying feathers
or tender raw fish,
if people canoeing
is your kind of meal,
being a crocodile
just might appeal to you.

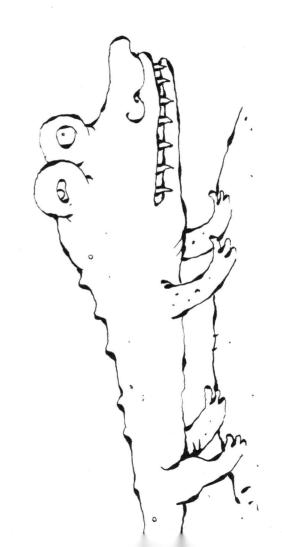

The sound of a toad
in the road
in the mud
is a soft sort of thump
and a very wet thud.

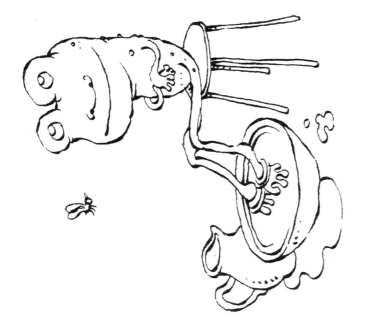

A frog's dream

is a green dream.

His bed is a stone pool bed.

The water warbles

the water flows

around his rubbery, webbery toes

while a jewel fly skims

his frogelegant nose

and the dream gleams green in his head.

Over a stone

under a fern

over an aphid

under an aster

slight hops

light hops

scant hops

grand hops

slow hops

low hops

long

strong

faster.

Flick, snap, gulp, swallow

beetle, bug and fly

in a wet green bog or hollow

quicker than an eye can follow

quicker than a fly can sigh.

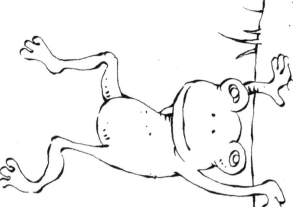

I am a creature

that hops on its hands

sits on its feet

squats as it stands.

Over and under

under and over

beeplant and bellwort

creamcups and clover.

Startings

partings

trips and stops

the toad's ways

and the toad's days

are the ways and days

of hops.

I am a snake.

I snake alone

though rushes and bushes

past moss and stone.

I slide though grass,

the slim stalks sigh,

bees buzz the news

as I slip by.

Mushrooms tremble,

clover tumbles,

one slight fieldmouse squeaks

and stumbles.

Butterflies and bees and bumbles
wing away to nests and hives,
beetles scatter for their lives.
Silence settles where I wend.
The snake is slow to make a friend.

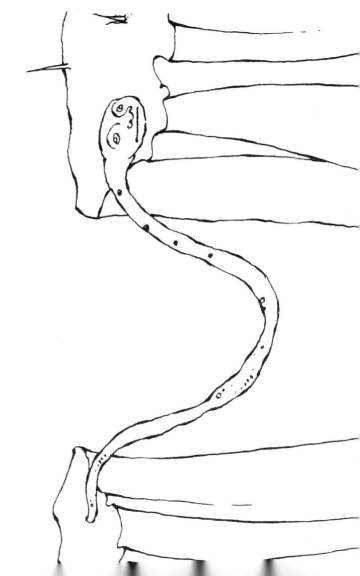

F

rom portal to portal
trudges the turtle.
It startles a toadstool
and treads through the myrtle.
It stops here and there
to speak to a stone.
The turtle's a mortal
who doesn't much chortle
from portal to portal
he turtles alone.

A snake slipped through the thin green grass

a silver snake
I watched it pass

it moved like a ribbon

silent as snow.

I think it smiled

as it passed my toe.

Bears Don't Purrr, They Grrrr

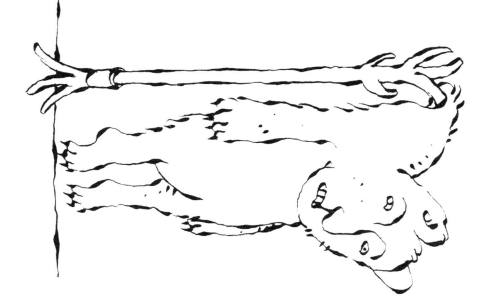

The bear coat
is a hair coat,
a coat of fur
to make bears purrr.
But bears don't purrr.
They grrrrr.

Long ago
there was a bear
with ice-blue eyes
and golden hair
and pale-pink paws
a bright black nose,
and a shiny, silken ribbon
more red than rose.

. . .

But though he was a perfect bear,
he had one secret, deep despair:
he did not have a thing to wear
except a lot of golden hair.

"I wish,"
he'd sigh,
"I had a pair
of socks or shoes
in reds or blues.
Some pale-plaid pants

"I'd also choose."
For hours he would sit and muse
on splendid clothes
that he would wear
were he not such a fair-haired bear.

· ·

One Wednesday
also long ago,
this gold-haired bear
went to and fro
to see the spring
and sniff the bud,
when Amelia Ellen Whitely,
who was holding him quite tightly,
tripped a little more than slightly
and he fell into the mud.

· · ·

Amelia Ellen had to stare.
There lay her once-so-golden bear
now muddied up from here to there.

· ·

Now muddied down from there to here,
from toe to toe
to ear to ear
to heel to heel
to knee to nose;
his ribbon hanging limply down,
a wet and brackish
blackish brown,
a lot more mud than rose.

• • •

She took him home
and ran the tub
and started in to soap and scrub,
to comb and brush,
to rinse and rub.
From dusk she worked
into the dawn,
and as the sunlight lit the lawn
no mud was there upon her bear.
But, oh,
Amelia had to stare,
his hair was also gone.

• • •

Then, her needle threaded tightly,

Amelia Ellen Whitely

stitched with energy and care

daily, noon, and nightly.

She made bear pairs

of socks and shoes

in rosey reds and azure blues,

jackets,

gloves,

and pale-plaid pants

at which each passerby would glance,

exclaiming with approving "oh's."

"I say, my dear,

do give a stare

at yonder very-well-dressed bear.

If I but had such splendid clothes."

.   .   .

Long ago

there was a bear

without a single golden hair.

He also did not have a care.

Oh, happy hair-free carefree bear.

A bear went walking
down the street
and everyone that bear did meet
that bear did greet
and also eat.
How sweet.

Compare the bears.

This one has hairs.

This one has none.

Come,

pair the bears.

Koala means the world to her.

His nose and paws are getting bald.

Koala, whispered in his ear,

is the only name he's called.

I cannot guess why he's preferred

to all the others sitting by—

the pandas, teddies, foreign dolls.

Koala has a missing eye.

He's made of fur.

Perhaps because he is so soft

she keeps him near.

There is a secret that she sees

that I don't see in him

that's clear.

Koala means the world to her.

A porcupine looks somewhat silly.

He also is extremely quilly

and if he shoots a quill at you

run fast

or you'll be quilly too.

"Cow" sounds heavy.

Cow

standing in the meadow

chewing.

A big fur box on legs

mooing.

What do you do for a living, my dear?

I'm a squirrel

leap and run

tree to tree

roof to roof

roof to tree in the sun.

Here to there

up to down

brownish grey

greyish brown

fence to limb

limb to roof

roof to gutter, pipe, wall

never once

never . . . once

never . . . .

. . . once through it all

will I flop, drop or tumble

scramble or fumble

topple or stumble

trip, plop or sprawl

or in any way . . . . .

fall.

I'm swimming around in the sea, see.
And the sea belongs to me, see.
I'm bigger and stronger
than fifteen
or twenty
and if you want trouble
then I'll give you plenty.

A sailboat and a chief of state
blew by and honked a bit too loud.
Now no one pushes me around
we whales are large and also proud.
I spouted once
and then I ate
the sailboat
and the chief of state.

So

I recommenced swimming

around in the sea

and spouting about its belonging to me

when a huge ocean liner

went by at a pace

that left me with ocean all over my face.

I gave a short spout at the shock

and the sound

but I stayed where I was.

As a whale I have found

it is my sea

until something bigger's around.

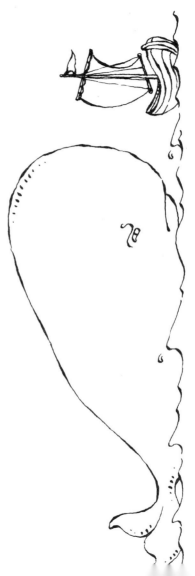

There was a hog
who ate a dog
and then he ate
a grass-green frog
and then he was so full
he cried.
And then he lay down—
bang—
and died.

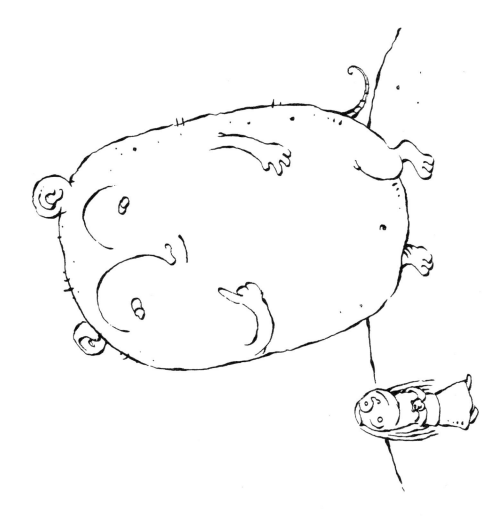

I would like to have a pet,
any kind will do.
I would like to have a pet
exactly like you.

Spring Again, Spring Again, Spring . . .

Spring again

spring again

spring again

isn't it?

Buds on the branches

a breeze in the blue

and me without mittens

my sweater unbuttoned

a spring full of things

all before me to do.

I'm shouting
I'm singing
I'm swinging through trees
I'm winging sky-high
with the buzzing black bees.
I'm the sun
I'm the moon
I'm the dew on the rose.
I'm a rabbit
whose habit
is twitching his nose.
I'm lively
I'm lovely
I'm kicking my heels.

I'm crying "Come dance"
to the freshwater eels.

I'm racing through meadows

without any coat

I'm a gamboling lamb

I'm a light leaping goat

I'm a bud

I'm a bloom

I'm a dove on the wing.

I'm running on rooftops

and welcoming spring!

Within a wood

I simply stood,

my thoughts as deep as wells.

I did not hear the sweet bird song.

I did not hear the bells

spring ringing through

the valleyed hills

from tree to tree to tree.

I did not hear the

windy, haunted rushing of the sea.

I did not hear the light leaves fall

and whisper to the ground.

I did not hear a thing

because there wasn't any sound.

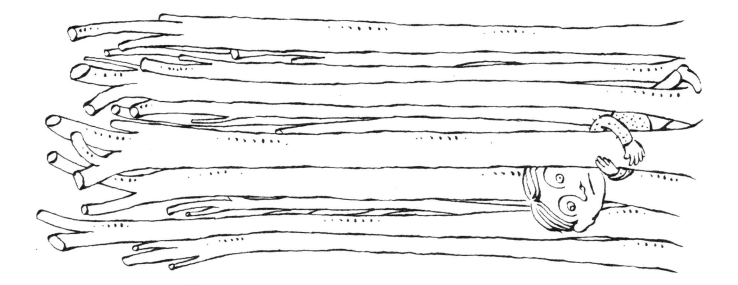

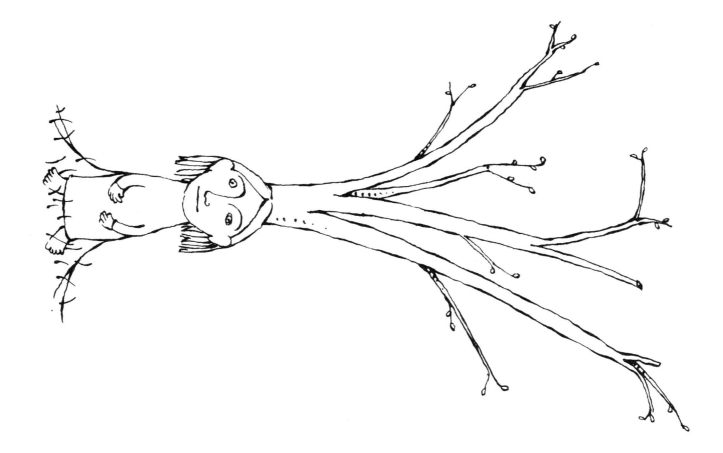

If you stood with your feet in the earth
up to your ankles in grass
and your arms had leaves running over them
and every once in a while one of your leafy fingers
was nudged by a bird flying past,
if the skin that covers you from top to tip
wasn't skin at all, but bark
and you never moved your feet from their place
in the earth
but stood rooted in that one spot come

rain

wind

snow

sleet

thaw

spring

summer

winter

fall

blight

bug

day

dark

then you would be me:
a tree.

I'm up here.
You're down there.
And nothing in that space between us
but a mile of air.
Where I sail:
clouds pass.
Where you run:
green grass.
Where I float:
birds sing.
One thin thing there is
that holds us close together:
kite string.

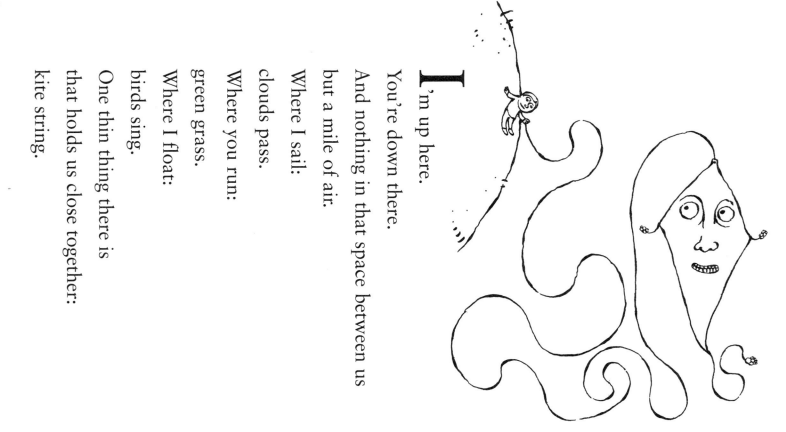

The flower's on the bird
which is underneath the bee
and the bird is on the kitten
on the cat on me.
I'm on a chair
on some grass
on a lawn
and the lawn is on a meadow
and the world is what it's on.
And all of us together
when the day is nearly done
like to sit and watch the weather
as we spin around the sun.

There's a tree by the meadow
by the sand by the sea
on a hillock near a valley
that belongs to me
with small spring leaves
like small green dimes
that cast their shadows on the grass
a thousand separate times
with round brown branches
like outstretched sleeves
and the twigs come out as fingers
and the fingers hold the leaves
with blossoms here and there
and always pink and soft and stout
and when the blossoms disappear
the apples hurry out
and
in the middle of the blossoms
in the center of the tree
with a hat and coat of leaves on
sits smiling me.

O ut to walk,
dog and I
raced the clouds,
saw the sky
blowing by,
grey with rain.
Dog and I
raced home again.

Dog and I
met some birds.
Dog barked,
birds chirped,
I spoke words.

Birds flew,
dog ran,
I walked home,
ate a cookie,
wrote a poem.

Five, Four,
Three, Too Hot!

Cats and dogs

it's hot out.

Rats and mice

it's hot.

Sun and stars

and Earth and Mars

it's five, four, three,

too hot!

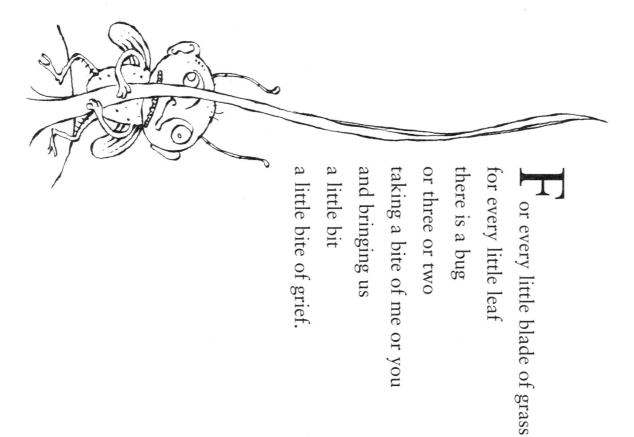

F or every little blade of grass
for every little leaf
there is a bug
or three or two
taking a bite of me or you
and bringing us
a little bit
a little bite of grief.

Heat, heat, heat,

the heat of it,

the pulse, the pound, the beat of it.

The flat, fat, hot of it.

The threatening sweat of it.

The un-sweet, perspiring wet of it.

It's no summer lull—

lullaby

to sit on a stoop in the dark of a night in July

starless and still as an oven at midnight

and fry.

When the fields are in flower

the cards come out

on the floor

on the couch

on the sand, sand, sand.

And Jool and Em sit face-to-face

and each one holds a hand

hand, hand

(and the hand that holds that hand

is tanned).

Diamonds, clubs, hearts, spades.

Those two would play in the Everglades.

Spades, hearts, diamonds, clubs.

They'd shuffle on planes or trains or subs.

Spit, trump, war, rummy.

In Egypt they'd play with somebody's

    mummy.

In China they'd play on the China wall

over the summer

and into the fall.

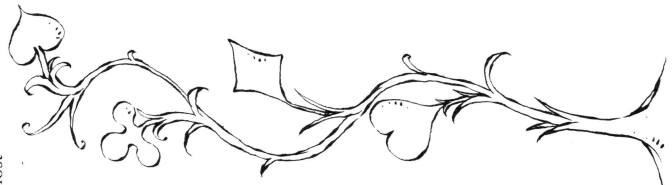

Shine, wind, rain, sun.
They play because they've lost
or won.
They play because
they are not done
with playing,
anyhow it's fun.
Sun, shine, wind, rain,
cut the cards
and begin again. . . .

Jack, queen, ace, ten
and again.

Dear shell,
you curve extremely well
and when I put you to my curving ear
and hear a whispered wind far off
I cannot tell but it might be
the sea.
Dear shell,
you also smell.

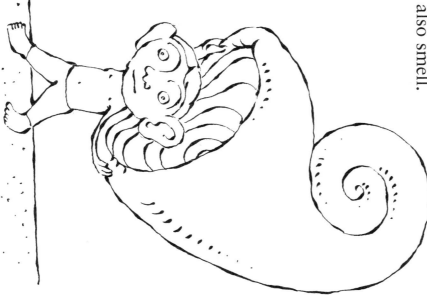

One hundred gulls were standing on the sand

when down the beach

walked Mrs. Dipper's daughter.

One hundred feet away

one hundred gulls

rose up

flew off

and sat down on the water.

This place began with yellow, green and blue,

a little red,

needles, scissors, thread.

A clever mother stitched the colors up.

The green for leaves and fields,

blue water

and the red that shades to brown

for roads that wander

down green valleys

over yellow hills

and end

like ribbons cut along the edge of blue.

Blue sea,

blue sky too.

She put her needle down

and bit the thread.

"Come see what I have made,"

she said,

"of yellow, red and blue.

A patchwork island, cut and sewed for you.

A place to play away long days

until the fields are mowed,

until the summer's through.

And then

at night we'll use it as a quilt

to cover you in bed.

These island nights can grow quite cool,"

she said.

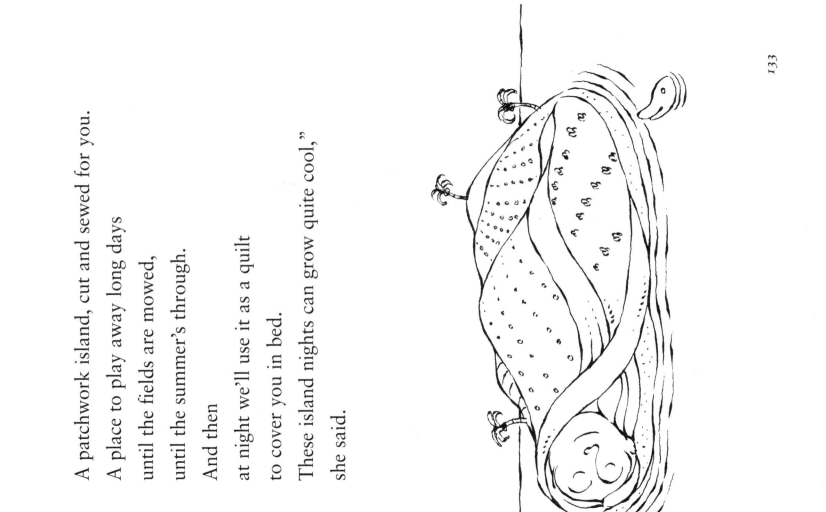

Don't frown
take the world and turn it upside down.
Take the down
and turn it upside world.
On days like this it is not difficult to do
the sea becomes the sky
a single blue
the fields are seaweed
under clouds of foam
fish feathers dip and shine
slim birds swim home.

A lot of summer by the sea

with Jool

(that's you)

and me

(that's me)

and sand

(quite hot)

and water

(not)

and pots

(of fish)

and fields

(of clover)

and days

(and days)

to play

(and laze)

and laze

(and play)

until fall comes

(and summer's over).

U nder the waves the mermaids lounge
eating ferns and sipping sea.
They comb the rippled wavelets of their hair
and smile most moistly.
Merdogs bark.
Mercats purr
on mermats in the sun.
The merbirds fly from here to mer.
The mermice squeak and run.
Close by the scalloped waves we walk
and scuff the sand and sniff the air,
unconscious of a merworld
close, close enough to touch

if it were there.

There are reaches of beaches

with nothing but sand

where you go with a shovel

a pail and a friend

and you dig there together

well into the winter

the summer

the autumn

the former

the latter.

Years pass and you leave

walking off hand in hand.

It doesn't much matter

how long you both dig there,

the sand will not end.

Sitting in the sand and the sea comes up

so you put your hands together

and you use them like a cup

and you dip them in the water

with a scooping kind of motion

and before the sea goes out again

you have a sip of ocean.

Uncountable billions
of small grains of stone

make a short stretch of beach

one can lie on alone

or dig landlocked lakes in

or castles or forts.
Uncountable billions
of small grains of quartz.

Young Miss Annabella Peach,

shovel, spoon and pail,

dug a cellar in the sand

that a passing whale

wants to rent until September,

it is just that big.

Sand's the stuff that holes are made of,

if you like to dig.

The stones that Annabella found

are worn by water

smooth and round.

She also has bright shells,

some snails,

small bits of boats,

old planks and nails,

and seaweed

that she's going to wear,

as mermaids do,

twined in her hair.

Sloping
slipping
sliding
gliding

Anna down the dunes is riding.
Sand dust flies before her eyes
while a windy, wet, watery roar
is all that she hears
as she rapidly nears
the edge of the sea slapped shore.

A turtle walks across the lawn
and when he gets there
summer's gone.

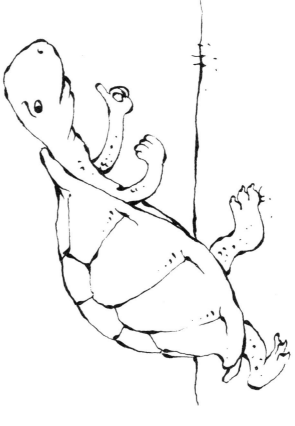

At the beginning:
unending clover.
When it's ended:
the geese fly over.

Good-bye Toes

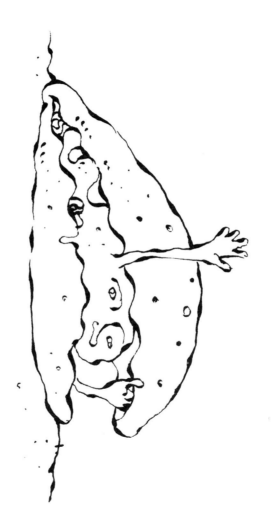

G ood-bye toes

shorts

tan

gulls

waves

wet sand.

So long knees

bathing suit

cliffs

capes

barley

oats

corn

clams

mackerel boats.

Good-bye sailing

sunsets

clover

cooking on the beach.

All over.

Bees

fields

picking berries

sea glass

dune grass

good-bye ferry

house

lane

warm rain.

So long sky.

When we come back next July

those trees will be a little taller.

So will I.

So long summer.

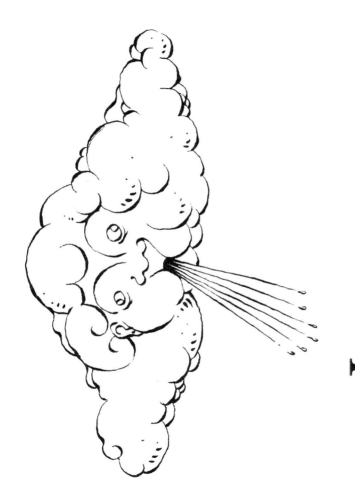

Look out of the window.
Listen to the wind blow.
Outside in
and inside out,
listen to the wild wind shout.

When I go walking in the fall
I stop to watch the deer.
They open up their lovely eyes
and blink
and disappear.
The rabbits hop from here
to there
and in
and out
and under
while deep within the forest heart
the black bears roar like thunder.
The chipmunks gather butternuts
and hide them in a tree
where clever squirrels
discover them
and laugh with squirrelish glee.

My hat is green
my jacket blue
with patches on the sleeves

and as I walk
I crunch through piles
of red and yellow leaves.

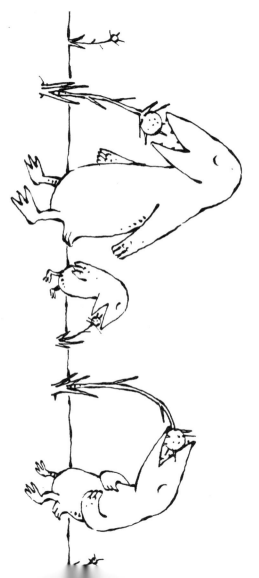

T hirty thirsty thistles
thicketed and green
growing in a grassy swamp
purple-topped and lean
prickly and thistly
topped by tufts of thorns
green mean little leaves on them
and tiny purple horns
briary and brambly
a spikey, spiney bunch of them.
A troop of bright red birds came by
and had a lovely lunch of them.

When I went out to see the sun

there wasn't sun or anyone

but there was only sand and sea

and lots of rain that fell on me

and where the rain and river met

the water got completely wet.

Days that the wind takes over
blowing through the gardens
blowing birds out of the street trees
blowing cats around corners
blowing my hair out
blowing my heart apart
blowing high in my head
like the sea sound caught in a shell.
One child put her thin arms around the wind
and they went off together.
Later the wind came back
alone.

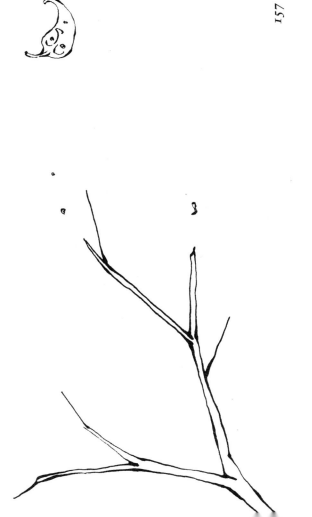

The leaves have left without a warning

I noticed when I woke this morning.

The spring arrived and then it went.

The summer came and now it's spent.

The leaves turned yellow, crimson, brown

and drifted, sifted slowly down.

And now the trees look bare and thin

it's time for winter to begin

and make their branches thick with snow

because that's how the seasons go.

Ice Is Nice

In winter there is too much ice.

In summer
ice is very nice.

Under my hood I have a hat
and under that
my hair is flat.
Under my coat
my sweater's blue.
My sweater's red.
I'm wearing two.
My muffler muffles to my chin
and round my neck
and then tucks in.
My gloves were knitted
by my aunts.
I've mittens too
and pants
and pants
and boots
and shoes
with socks inside.

The boots are rubber, red and wide.
And when I walk
I must not fall
because I can't get up at all.

I am softer

and colder

and whiter than you.

And I can do something

that you cannot do.

I can make anything

anything

beautiful:

warehouses

train tracks

an old fence

cement.

I can make anything

everything

beautiful.

What I touch,

where I blow,

even a dump filled with garbage

looks lovely

after I've fallen there.

I am the snow.

Summer is gone

and so are the roses.

Sidewalks are icy

and so are our noses.

Noses are rosy

and so are our cheeks

and will be for many long

wintery weeks.

W hen you open your mouth
the snow snows in.
The flakes are fat
and flat and thin
and some of them land
on your nose
and chin.

Flake upon
flake upon
flake
makes a snowdrift.
Each icy pattern like no other one.
Numberless crystals
that cover the roofs
and the roads
and the valleys
and melt in the sun.

W hen it is dry

I cry.

The rain is a pest and a pain.

When I see flowers

growing red and high

I hope they will die in their flower bed.

I

am a sled.

It's snowing
and snowing
so what shall we eat?
The snow looks so good
I will make you a treat.
I'm a very fine cook
and I have what it takes.
Come into the kitchen.
I'm baking some flakes.

For wandering walks
in the sparkling snow
no one is muffled
more warmly than Joe.
No one is mittened more
coated or hatted
booted or sweatered
both knitted and tatted
buttoned and zippered
tied, tucked and belted
padded and wadded
and quilted and felted
hooked in and hooded
tweeded and twilled.
Nothing of Joe's
from his top to his toes
but the tip of his nose

could be touched
by the snows
or the wind as it blows
and grow rather rosy
the way a nose grows
if it's frozen
or possibly chilled.

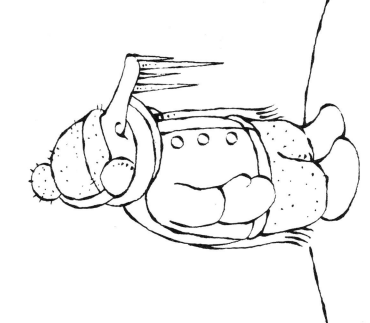

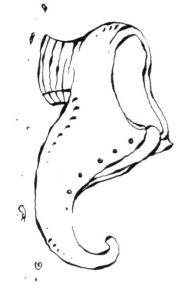

I'm scratched and scuffed.
The socks have holes.
The sidewalk's hard.
I hate the shoves
when boots go on.
One lace is gone.
I sometimes wish that I were gloves.

I t's rotten

when there's two of you

bright red and warm

and then they lose

the other one

and I get wet.

It makes me wish that I were shoes.

A tiny house,
a Christmas tree
within a round glass globe
and me.
The house is cookie color brown.
The tree: deep green,
and I am so
amazed to see us upside down
and covered suddenly with snow.

The tree has leaves
and I have hair.
In winter
when the tree is bare,
I wear a hat
to warm my head
and keep my ears
from turning red.

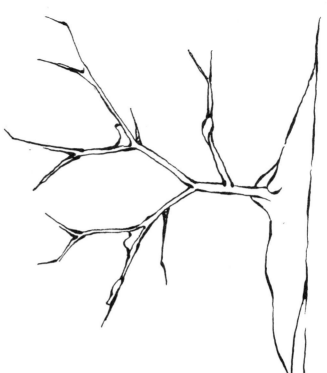

We'll play in the snow
and stray in the snow
and stay in the snow
in a snow-white park.
We'll clown in the snow
and frown in the snow
fall down in the snow
till it's after dark.
We'll cook snow pies
in a big snow pan.
We'll make snow eyes
in a round snow man.
We'll sing snow songs
and chant snow chants
and roll in the snow
in our fat snow pants.
And when it's time to go home to eat
we'll have snow toes
on our frosted feet.

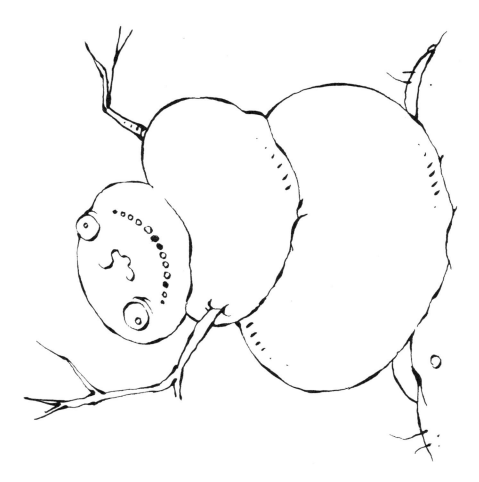

A boy had a mother who bought him a hat,

red as a rose
and it kept off the snows.
He loved it so much
that whatever he did
or whatever he said
he wore his new hat
which was woolly and red.
He stood in a wood
in his hat,
on his head.

So then she went out and she bought him a mouse.
Sniffing and squeaking
and seeking and peeking.

He loved it so much
that whatever he did
or whatever he said
when dressed in his hat

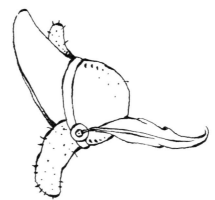

which was woolly and red,
he included his mouse.
And he built it a small
very comfortable house
which he painted sky blue.
He went to a party.
The mouse went there too.

Well then she went out and she bought him
 new shoes,
brown ones with laces for going to places.

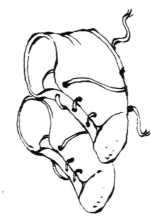

He loved them so much
that whatever he did
or whatever he said
when dressed in his hat
which was woolly and red,

while holding his mouse
in its house of sky blue,
he wore his two shoes
which were shiny and new.
They looked very dashing
and dapper on him
when he walked to the seashore
and went for a swim.

After that she went out and she bought him
      new boots,
a black rubber pair like the firemen wear.

He loved them so much
that whatever he did
or whatever he said
when dressed in his hat
which was woolly and red,
while holding his mouse
in its house of sky blue,
and wearing his shoes

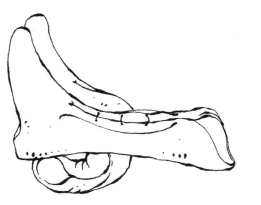

which were hidden
but new,
he did with his boots on.
No reason to laugh
except that he wore them
while taking a bath.

The next day she bought him some very nice skis,
waxed to a glow to cut tracks through the snow.

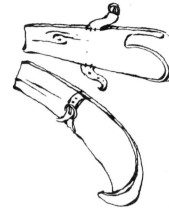

He loved them so much
that whatever he did
or whatever he said
when dressed in his hat
which was woolly and red,
while holding his mouse
in its house of sky blue,
and wearing his shoes
which were very new too,
he did with his skis on,
and though a beginner

he wore them one night
to his Grandma's for dinner.

On Halloween evening she bought him a mask.
It made him quite merry to look very scary.

He loved it so much
that whatever he did
or whatever he said
when dressed in his hat
which was woolly and red,
while holding his mouse
in its house of sky blue,
and wearing his shoes
which were shiny and new,
hidden under his boots
which were very new too,
well strapped to his skis
which were yellow and bright,
from dawn until dusk
until noon until night,
he kept on his mask

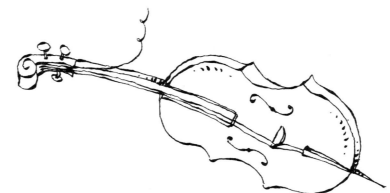

and looked ghostly or worse.
When he went to the doctor's
he frightened the nurse.

She went out one day and she bought him a cello.
You know you don't blow it.
To play it you bow it.

He loved it so much
that whatever he did
or whatever he said
when dressed in his hat
which was woolly and red,
while holding his mouse
in its house of sky blue,
and wearing his shoes
which were shiny and new,
hidden under his boots
which were pretty new too,
well strapped to his skis
which were polished and bright,
from dawn until dusk

until noon until night
with his Halloween mask
(very scary and yellow),
he NEVER let go
of his elegant cello.
He played away worry
and hurry and care;
he played for some rabbits,
five birds and a bear.

She went out once more and she bought him an
elephant.
But not just a small one—a heavy, grey, tall one.

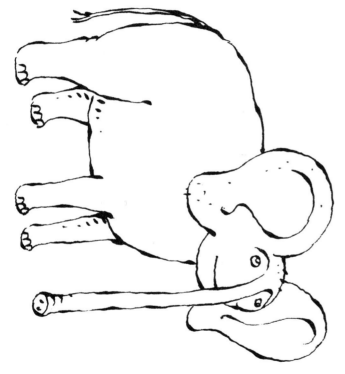

He loved it so much
that whatever he did
or whatever he said
when dressed in his hat
which was woolly and red,
while holding his mouse
in its house of sky blue,
and wearing his shoes
which were shiny and new,
hidden under his boots
which looked almost new too,
well strapped to his skis
which were polished and bright,
from dawn until dusk
until noon until night
with his Halloween mask
which was scary and yellow,
from summer through winter
embracing his cello,
his elephant went,
and they raced everywhere

until in a frost frozen flurry of air
his hat blew away
and it left his hair bare
to the wild windy roar.
Then his mother yelled,
"Dear, I am off to the store.
It is very clear that
you must have a new hat."
And she rushed out the door.

A boy had a mother who bought him a hat,
red as a rose
and it kept off the snows.

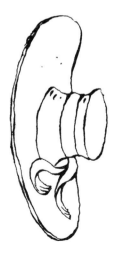

I'm sick of boots
and winter clothes.
I want to wear
just shorts and toes.

When weather's wild and winter cold
hand in mittened hand
two friends will race the windy beach
and watch snow
snow on sand.

S_{and}

or

snow?
I do not know
and leave it up to you.

I Will Not
Eat Beets

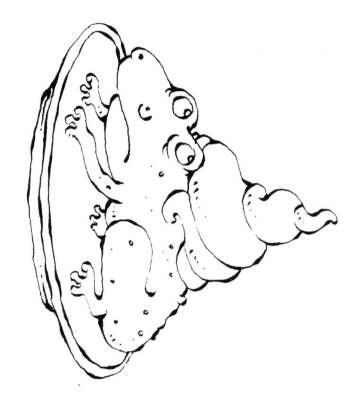

I will not eat beets.
I do not wish fish.
But I will have a little more
of that delicious dinosaur.
And for dessert I'll have the toad.
I think I'd like it à la mode.

Whether it's sleeting or raining or snowing raisins are perfect for eating and throwing.

If you were an onion
and I was an eye
I'd watch someone chop you
and wouldn't I cry?

M
Mice are very fond of it.
So's my Dad.
I think cheese is . . . .
often smelly,
blue and green and . . . .
not so bad.

Good morning, corn.

Please don't let me stop you.

Just grow up tall

and then I'm going to pop you.

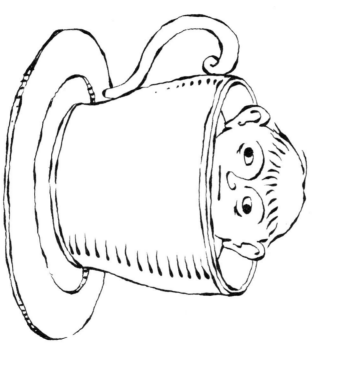

M om drinks tea
and Grandma does.
I'd rather have a cup of fuzz.

Some things you know
and don't need to be told:

the thing about milk is
it's wonderful cold.

But if it sits out in the heat of the sun

for hours on end

I would like to have none.

Take an iguana and bake it.
Don't bake an iguana,
just take it.
Take it to lunch
and buy it a bunch
of parsley or manna
and tell that iguana
you'll love it
and never forsake it.

Here's a shady glade of lunch trees

close beside a golden pool

(gold because it's apple cider)

golden sweet and icy cool.

Let us have a little picnic

underneath the sandwich tree.

Pick yourself that tuna salad.

Pick a ham and cheese for me.

Mayo from the mayo bush,

ketchup from the vine.

You can pick a peck of pickles but

that deviled egg is mine.

We will sit and sing and swallow

till the sun grows red and low

over this delicious meadow.

Then when it is time to go

we will watch some hungry ants

followed by their beetle chums

picnic in the shady glade there

sipping cider, picking crumbs.

202

I am making stew for you.
First I will put in a shoe.
Then I will put in some glue.
Then some dust
from off the floor.
Would you like a little more?

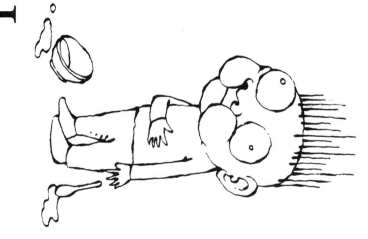

Liquid isn't solid.

Liquid is to drink.

If you do not like it

pour it down the sink.

Juice is lovely liquid,

orange, apple, pear.

Squeeze some fruit to fill a glass.

Then gulp, gulp, gulp,

ahhh . . . there.

Butter
butter
butter
butter
that's a word
I love to utter.

Chocolate

vanilla

coffee

and peach.

Let me have a cone of each.

When I am through

I will have some more.

Then I will fall down on the floor.

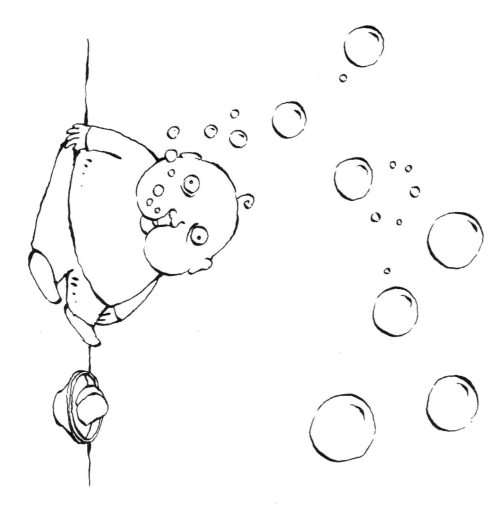

I am making soup
of soap.
James will drink it up
I hope.
I have not been friends with James
since he called me all those names.

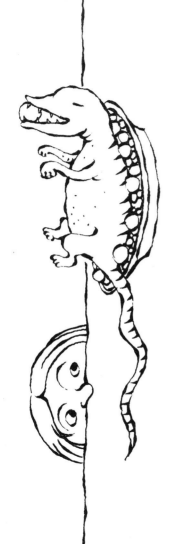

I have a hunch
I won't like lunch.

I liked growing.

That was nice.

The leaves were soft

the sun was hot.

I was warm and red and round

then someone dropped me in a pot.

Being a strawberry isn't all pleasing.

This morning they put me in ice cream.

I'm freezing.

Catherine said, "I think I'll bake
a most delicious chocolate cake."
She took some mud and mixed it up
while adding water from a cup
and then some weeds and nuts and bark
and special gravel from the park
a thistle and a dash of sand.
She beat out all the lumps by hand.
And on the top she wrote "To You"
the way she says the bakers do
and then she signed it "Fondly, C."
and gave the whole of it to me.
I thanked her but I wouldn't dream
of eating cake without ice cream.

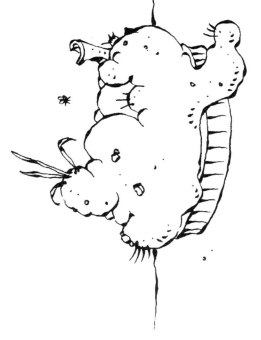

(Shortly after six o'clock
across the street and down the block,
sweet, insistent,
loud and clear
a nightly bell
beguiles my ear.)

Just last night
I had this dream:
the ice cream truck
was pure ice cream.
The wheels were chocolate,
that was nice,
the fenders all were orange ice.
The bumpers? Mint,
the doors were peach,
a coffee handle opened each.
The roof,
which was pistachio,
looked most of all like pale green snow

with bits of nuts.

The headlights shone

from deep within two sugar cones.

And in this dream I did not budge

but stood still

stunned

inhaling fudge.

When suddenly

from down the street

there was a rush of running feet

and countless mouths and hands and eyes,

every color,

any size.

Those eyes showed hunger and surprise.

Alerted by the bell's bright tune

feet ran

and each hand held a spoon.

I
said to my mommy,
"I'd like some salami."
My mommy said,
"Certainly honey,
that will be no bother
but wouldn't you rather
have eggs inside outside
or sunny?"
I murmured,
"Please Mommy
I just want salami.
A sandwich will suit me just fine."
Said she,
"Why not steak
in a cake wrapped in bacon
or take a few minutes and dine
on oysters au gratin
with eggplant?"

"Oh, ROTTEN"

I snapped very loud at my ma.

"I'm telling you Mommy

I just want salami."

Then Mom said,

"That's what it will be."

She sliced it up thickly.

We ate it up quickly.

"DELICIOUS"

yelled Mommy and me.

Timothy Tompkins had turnips and tea.
The turnips were tiny.
He ate at least three.
And then for dessert,
he had onions and ice.
He liked that so much
that he ordered it twice.
He had two cups of ketchup,
a prune and a pickle.
"Delicious," said Timothy.
"Well worth a nickel."
He folded his napkin and hastened to add,
"It's one of the loveliest breakfasts I've had."

T o eat an egg
and eat it right
first of all you eat the white.
Then you eat the yellow yolk.
Then you take your spoon
and poke
the awfully slipping, dripping stuff.
And then you yell,
"I've had enough."

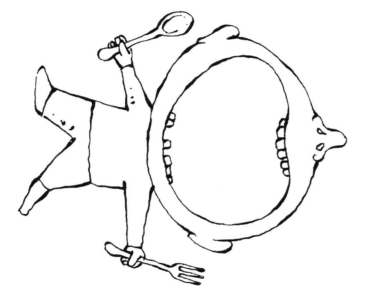

Thin or fat
fat or thin.
Open your mouth
and the food goes in.
And what you eat—
a bit of sweet,
a bite of stew—
each bite and bit
turns into you.

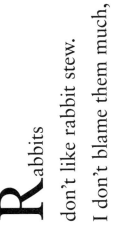

Rabbits
don't like rabbit stew.
I don't blame them much,
do you?

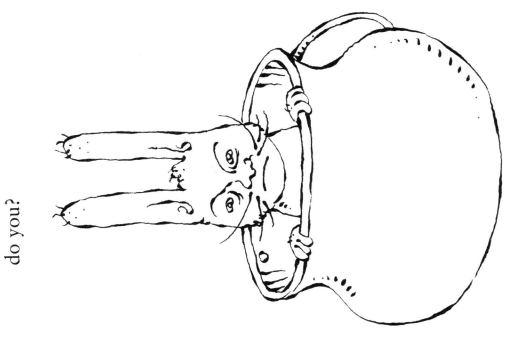

I Need to Read

I need to read.

It's a little like breathing

or eating

or drinking

my life's link to thinking.

Without it I am

much less than I am,

less of a person

and more of a yam.

Reading is writing

is learning

is growing

igniting cognition,

that's what keeps one going

trucking along on a civilized track

more upward than downward

and possibly forward,

it feels like it's forward,

most probably forward,

and forward

is generally better than back.

What separates each one of us
from all the beasts and bugs and birds?
Well they have feathers, fur and wings
but we have words,
and words,
and words.

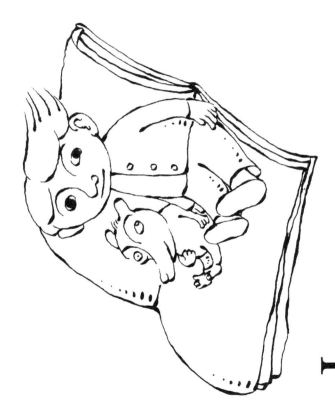

I know a way to open doors
and find adventure, tears and pleasure

where witches whisper,

frogs are men

and pirates on wild shores

call us to join a quest for untold treasure.

There

what we find depends on where we look.

A thousand worlds, or more, await us.

Travel with me,

come,

we'll go by the book.

Rain lifts my heart,
it always did.
On sunny days
good children fled
to be outside, but I,
a kid,
stayed in and read,
while all one's elders,
tall and grey,
said, "Darling, do go out and play."
And Darling shot them such a look,
from over some beloved book
that Mother, or some timid aunt
would turn,
without a word indeed,
to darn a sock, deadhead a plant
and leave me be
and let me read.
Rain was my ally and salvation
defending me from confrontation.

Curled in a chair,
my book and eye
delighted in a storming sky.
Thrilled to the wind's wet roar
or moan,
knowing I would be left alone.

Then picture this,
come Armageddon,
quite undisturbed
she sat and read on.

Where do you get the idea for a poem?

Does it shake you awake?

Do you dream it asleep

or into your tiny tin head does it creep

and pop from your pen

when you are not aware

or leap from your pocket

or fall from your hair

or is it just silently

suddenly

there?

In a beat

in a breath

in a pause

in a cry

one unblinking eye

that stares from the dark

that is deep in your head

demanding attention

until it is written

until it is rotten

until it is anything else but forgotten

until it is read.

Three wishes

three.
The first
a tree:

dark bark

green leaves

under a bit of blue

a canopy

to glimpse sky through

to watch sun sift through

to catch light rain

upon the leaves

and let it fall again.

A place to put my eye

beyond the window frame.

Wish two:

a chair

not hard or high

one that fits comfortably

set by the window tree

an island in the room

for me

my own

place to sit and be

alone.

My tree

there.

Here my chair,

me,

rain, sky, sun.

All my wishes

all the things I need

but one

wish three:

a book to read.

So I picked out a book
on my own
from the shelf
and I started to read
on my own
to myself.
And nonsense and knowledge
came tumbling out,
whispering mysteries,
history's shout,
the wisdom of wizards,
the songs of the ages,
all wonders of wandering
wonderful pages.

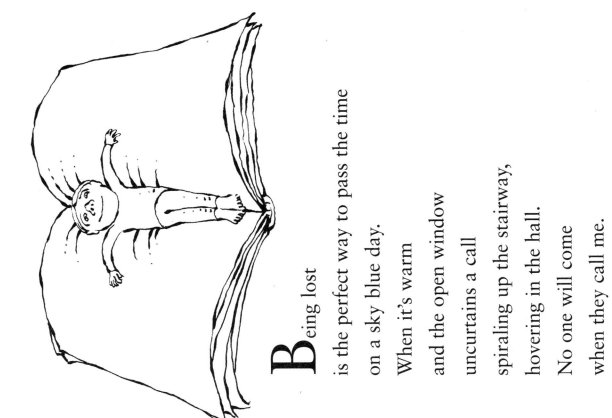

Being lost
is the perfect way to pass the time
on a sky blue day.

When it's warm
and the open window
uncurtains a call
spiraling up the stairway,
hovering in the hall.

No one will come
when they call me.
I am not there
where they look.

I linger alone in a place of my own,
lost in a book.

Dig deep in you.
Keep everything you find.
Sketch the ever-changing views
dappled behind your eyes,
rustling in your mind.
Unlock the weather
in your heart.
Unleash a thousand whispers,
let them shout.
Then,
when you feel
the presence
of a poem
waiting to spring
to sting
within you,
bewitch it
into words
and sing it out.

Remember books?

We read them with our eyes and minds.

We held them in our hands

sprawled out in chairs,

on beds,

on stomachs

or our small behinds.

And what we read

we lived in and we knew.

These were not disembodied words

afloat on some smooth manufactured

screen.

They sighed and spoke

and were a part of you.

There Is a Me
Inside of Me

There is a me inside of me,

inside

the outside me

you see.

I am beside myself
with glee.

I ho
and ho

and hee
and hee,

and hee
and ho

and ho.

I hee
and hee

I hee
and ho

and ho.

I wonder why
I'm ho-ing so.

People always say to me
"What do you think you'd like to be
when you grow up?"
And I say "Why,
I think I'd like to be the sky
or be a plane or train or mouse
or maybe be a haunted house
or something furry, rough and wild . . .
or maybe I will stay a child."

I woke up this morning
at quarter past seven.
I kicked up the covers
and stuck out my toe.
And ever since then
(that's a quarter past seven)
they haven't said anything
other than "no."

They haven't said anything
other than "Please, dear,
don't do what you're doing,"
or "Lower your voice."

Whatever I've done
and however I've chosen,
I've done the wrong thing
and I've made the wrong choice.

I didn't wash well
and I didn't say thank you.
I didn't shake hands
and I didn't say please.

I didn't say sorry
when passing the candy
I banged the box into
Miss Witelson's knees.

I didn't say sorry.
I didn't stand straighter.
I didn't speak louder
when asked what I'd said.
Well, I said
that tomorrow
at quarter past seven
they can
come in and get me.
I'm Staying In Bed.

Once there was a cyclops
who didn't wonder why-clops
but nodded
and assented to his fate.

He had one blue wistful eye-clops
and he'd sometimes sadly sigh-clops
and murmur he would like to have
a mate.

It is really very lonely
to forever be the only,
like a cyclops,
so he dried a single tear.

"Oh," he said,
"I would not cry-clops,
if I had a loved one nigh-clops
for a cyclops to this guy-clops
would bring cheer."

Well he met her quite soon after

and their lives are filled with laughter

and their hearts are filled with gladness

year by year,

since the day he whispered,

"Cyclops

please consent to just be my-clops."

And she answered sweetly,

"Fie-clops

have no fear.

From now on I am thy-clops

till we lie-clops down and die-clops,

standing by-clops sweetie-pie-clops

cyclops dear."

I do not laugh or sing or smile or talk.
I cannot count to ten.
My feet don't walk.
My hair is straight
it does not grow or curl,
I do not dance ballet
or eat a meal
but even so
there is a girl I know
who thinks I'm real.

Okay everybody, listen to this:

I am tired of being smaller

than you

and them

and him

and trees and buildings.

So watch out

all you gorillas and adults

beginning tomorrow morning

boy

am I going to be taller.

Where
have you been dear?
What
have you seen dear?
What
did you do there?
Who
went with you there?
Tell me
what's new dear?
What's
new with you dear?
Where
will you go next?
What
will you do?

"I do this and I do that.
I go here and I go there.
At times I like to be alone.
There are some thoughts that are my own
I do not wish to share."

Running away
from the rest of today
running away
from you
running away
from "Don't do that"
from all of the things
I must constantly do.
I feel too tall
I feel too old
for a hundred helpings of being told.
Packing my head
taking my feet
galloping down the familiar street.
My head is a bird.
My heart is free again.
I might come back
when I feel like me again.

What would you choose
if you were free
to be anything fat
that you wanted to be?
Anything thin or long or tall,
anything red, blue, black, at all;
a bird on the wing
or a fish on the fin?
If you're ready to choose
it is time to begin.

. . .

If you could be square
would you be a box
containing a cake
or a house
or blocks
with painted letters
from A to Z?
Who would you
which would you
what would you be?

If you could be soft
would you be the snow
or twenty-five pillows
or breezes that blow
the blossoms that fall from
the sassafras tree?
Who would you
which would you
what would you be?

    . . .

If you could be loud
would you be the sound
of thunder at night
or the howl of a hound
as he bays at the moon
or the pound of the sea?
Who would you
which would you
what would you be?

    . . .

If you could be small
would you be a mouse
or a mouse's child
or a mouse's house
or a mouse's house's
front door key?
Who would you
which would you
what would you be?

. . .

If you could be dark
would you be the night
or a house on a hill
where there wasn't a light
or a witch watcher
watching a witch with glee?
Who would you
which would you
what would you be?

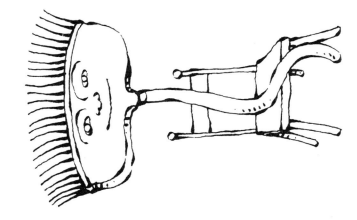

My world is an enormous room
with dust upon the floor.
It sometimes makes me wonder
if there is nothing more to life
than sweeping dust around a room?
Now if I were a *witch's* broom . . .

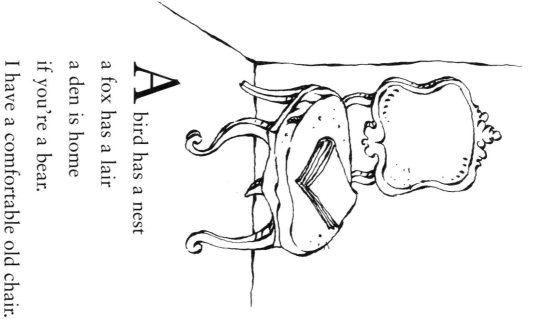

A bird has a nest
a fox has a lair
a den is home
if you're a bear.
I have a comfortable old chair.

Soft pillowed blue,
a flowered cloud.

The perfect place to read aloud

to myself or silently

letting long words run over me,

letting the stories I have read

make moving pictures in my head.

New chairs are fine

but mine is best.

My spot to think in

brood in

rest

to plot in

dream in, many dreams,

to scheme a few outlandish schemes in.

Kings need crowns to be the king

but me

I can be anything

any person,

anywhere,

if I just have my book and chair.

I'm sitting on an old cold star,

me and a lot of stones.

Not a tree or a bird

or a chair.

I'm looking out across an endless curve of sky

across an empty universe of air

to where my world spins

tree green,

sea blue,

there.

City, windows, house and room,

crayons, bike, bed, book and bear

there.

Snug

and VERY

far

far

far

away.

Dear Earth,

I miss your green and blue.

I miss my room and bear.

It's dull and lonely here on this old star.

I miss your night, Dear Earth,

the moon above,

the cool dark grass below.

I miss each always-different, ever-changing day.

You know the way you are, Dear Earth.

Well, stay that way.

The house of snail upon his back
protects from weather and attack
though just who might attack a snail
is a question I must fail to answer.

The turtle in his turtle shell
is shell-tered well.
The only skin that shows a bit
on him
is nose and toes a bit
on him.

I have a blue coat with a hood
like a private tent or roof
water, every weather proof.
Warm, secure
a snuggery
it often walks around with me.

A home away when I'm away

letting all the stars in

keeping out the damp grey.

True

good

blue

hood

it suits me well

my shell.

It is grey out.

It is grey in.

In me

it is as grey as the day is grey.

The trees look sad

and I,

not knowing why I do,

cry.

There is a bed
inside my head
and when the day is long
I curl within
my outside skin
and sing myself a song.

I'm very good at climbing
I nearly climbed a tree
but just as I was almost up
I sort of skinned my knee.

I'm wonderful at walking
I almost walked a mile
but when I got around the block
I rested for a while.

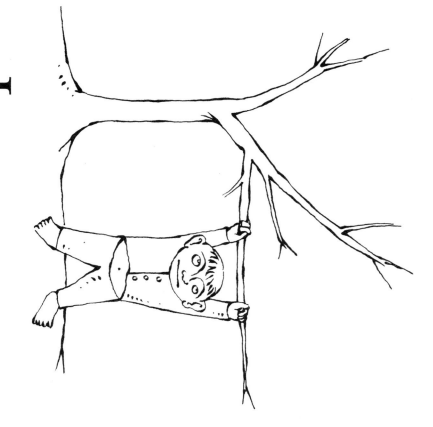

I'm excellent at swimming
though I'm not very old
I almost swam the ocean
but the water was too cold.

But what I'm really best at
is skipping down the hall.
I'm very good at skipping.
I'm wonderful at skipping.
I'm marvelous at skipping,
that is unless I fall.

D o not jump on ancient uncles.

Do not yell at average mice.

. . .

Do not wear a broom to breakfast.

. . .

Do not ask a snake's advice.

. . .

Do not bathe in chocolate pudding.

. . .

Do not talk to bearded bears.

. . .

Do not smoke cigars on sofas.

. . .

Do not dance on velvet chairs.

. . .

Do not take a whale to visit
Russell's mother's cousin's yacht.

. . .

And whatever else you do do
it is better you
do not.

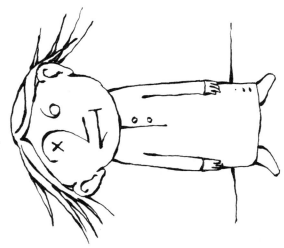

Is six times one a lot of fun?

Or eight times two?

Perhaps for you.

But five times three

unhinges me,

while six and seven and eight times eight

put me in an awful state

and four and six and nine times nine

make me want to cry and whine

so when I get to twelve times ten

I begin to wonder when

I can take a vacation from multiplication

and go out

and start playing again.

There is a tree
that grows in me.
A tree that no one else can see.

There is a bird upon the tree
upon the tree
that grows in me.
The tree that no one else can see.

And when the bird
upon the tree
begins to sing
you think it's me.

The sky is always in the sky,

the land is on the land.

The sea stays where

the sea should stay.

The world is nicely planned.

Brooks do not run in riverbeds.

The flower does not grow

into a spreading chestnut tree.

Corn doesn't peck the crow.

For if it did

or was

or were

it's obvious to see,

I might have been an elephant,

you might have been a me.

But I am me,

the tree's a tree,

likewise the plant's a plant.

And you are as you always were,

my dearest elephant.

Isn't It Queer
That an Ear
Can Hear?

Isn't it queer
that an ear
can hear?

These are my knees.
My knees are bony places
that bend when I am walking
down the block
or running races.

I look like you precisely.

You

clean and combed

washed well

and dressed up nicely.

But I am paper flat and under glass

showing you smiling

standing in your class

while you are jumping up to shout

"That's me!"

which isn't altogether true.

In fact it's really me you see.

I am a photograph of you.

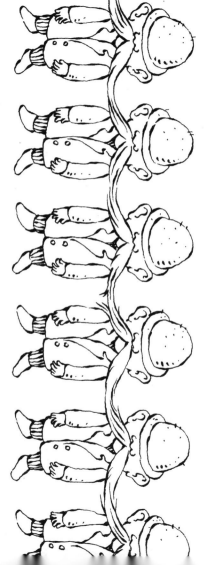

The streets are filled with mustached men

looking like each other

who?

The streets

are filled with mustached men

looking like each other

who?

The

streets

are filled with mustached men

looking like each other

who?

The streets are

filled

with mustached men

looking like each other

who?

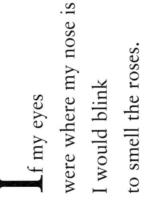

I f my eyes
were where my nose is
I would blink
to smell the roses.

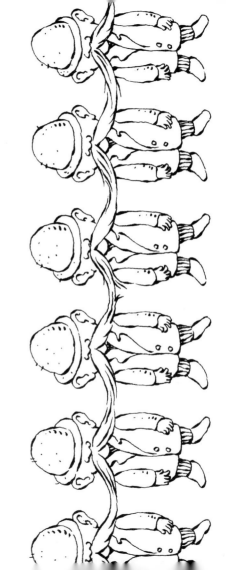

Hughbert had a jar of glue.
From Hugh the glue could not be parted,
at least could not be parted far,
for Hugh was glued to Hughbert's jar.
But that is where it all had started.
The glue upon the shoe of Hugh
attached him to the floor.
The glue on Hughbert's gluey hand
was fastened to the door,
while two of Hughbert's relatives
were glued against each other.
His mother, I believe, was one.
The other was his brother.
The dog and cat stood quite nearby.
They could not move from there.
The bird was glued securely
into Hughbert's mother's hair.

Hughbert's father hurried home
and loudly said to Hugh:

"From now on I would rather
that you did not play with glue."

This is my foot.
My foot is mine
and that is true.
I know because
my foot is in my shoe.
Or does that foot belong to you?
Then what's it doing in my shoe?

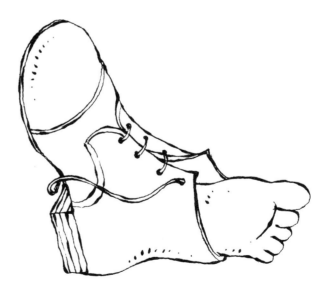

There was a man who was so fat
he wore a bathtub for a hat.

He wore a basin for a shoe,
and if you do not think this true
you've but to look across the square.
You see those mountains standing there
between the sky-blue sky and lawn?
Well, one has got a bathtub on.

The outside me
(the me you see)
begins with skin.
And there
above my chin
beneath my hair:
one mouth
a nose
two eyes
and ears
that let the outside in.

Some of us float
and some of us sink
and I am one who sinks
I think.
If I were a mermaid's
fishtailed daughter
I never would sink
in my home of water.

Once upon
upon a time
there was a child
who spoke in rhyme.

Three tall physicians and a nurse
have testified
that it was verse.

His hair was brown.
His height was short.
His pants were grey,
the shorter sort.

His name was Alexander Soames
and when he spoke
he spoke in poems.

• • •

The first time Alex saw a cat
he did not run,
he simply sat
and said,

"It's flat
that that's
a cat."

. . .

And when he saw a dog he said,
scratching his small poetic head,
"The walk of a dog
is more a jog
and less of a dance
than the amble of ants."

. . .

Alexander had a mother.
"Dear," she said a thousand times,
"dear," she said to Alexander,
"must you always speak in rhymes?
Wear your rubbers,
wipe your nose,
why not try
to speak in prose?"

. . .

"I prefer," said Alex Soames,

"to speak the speech I speak

in poems."

Alexander first walked this way.

Alexander then walked that.

"Rhyming suits me," Alex murmured,

"I suit rhyming," and he sat,

sat and pondered,

sat and sat.

. . .

"I will try once more," said Alex,

"I'll attempt it though I tend

to have doubts about the outcome.

Here's a simple phrase:

The End."

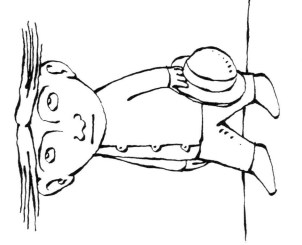

My head is here.

My hat is there.

My head sits underneath

my hair.

My hair sits underneath

my hat.

And that is why

my hair lies flat.

T here was a witch who knitted things:
Elephants and playground swings.
She knitted rain,
she knitted night,
but nothing really came out right.
The elephants had just one tusk
and night looked more
like dawn or dusk.
The rain was snow
and when she tried
to knit an egg
it came out fried.
She knitted birds
with buttonholes
and twenty rubber butter rolls.
She knitted blue angora trees.

She purl stitched countless purple fleas.
She knitted a palace in need of a darn.
She knitted a battle and ran out of yarn.
She drew out a strand
of her gleaming, green hair
and knitted a lawn
till she just wasn't there.

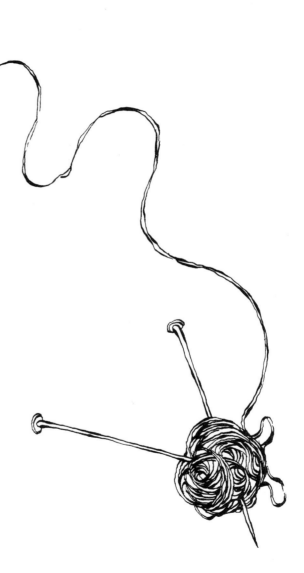

I am standing on the sand.
All my toes are here.
I can see each one because
the water is so clear.

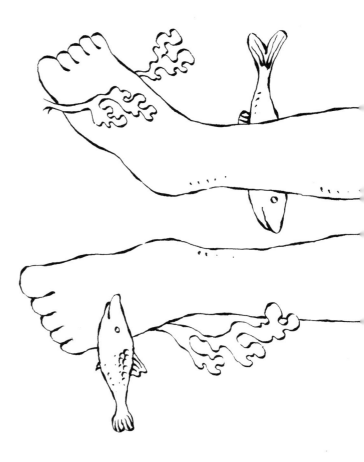

My nose is blue,

my teeth are green,

my face is like a soup tureen.

I look just like a lima bean.

I'm very, very lovely.

My feet are far too short

and long.

My hands are left and right

and wrong.

My voice is like the hippo's song.

I'm very, very,

very, very,

very, very

lovely?

Moon, Have You Met My Mother?

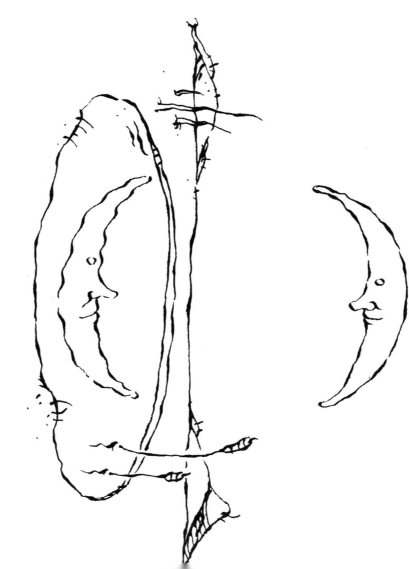

Moon,
have you met my mother?
Asleep in a chair there
falling down hair.

Moon in the sky
moon in the water
have you met one another?
Moon face to moon face
deep in that dark place
suddenly bright.

Moon,
have you met my friend the night?

Write about a radish
too many people write about the moon.

The night is black
the stars are small and high
the clock unwinds its ever-ticking tune
hills gleam dimly
distant nighthawks cry.
A radish rises in the waiting sky.

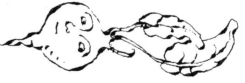

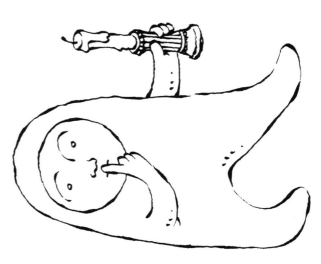

When everything has drawn to a close,

when games are done

and friends are gone from sight

you

and the tired mice

the nesting rabbits

go to your sleep

as I put out the light.

I'm night.

To count myself
is quickly done.
There's never more of me
than one.

. . .

Counting bears
is fun by ones
but funnier in pairs.

. . .

Counting socks
can be terribly hard
until you find you've lost one
on the stairs
or in the yard.

. . .

Counting caterpillars
as they climb the stalks of flowers
is easily accomplished
if you're free for many hours.

. . .

Counting the birds
on the branches of trees
is hard on the neck
but it's easy on the knees.

• • •

It's even harder
counting leaves
than counting tiny birds.
They shift their shadows
with the breeze
among the branches
of the trees
more numerous
than whispered words.

• • •

Counting fingers
and counting toes is
a harder kind of counting
than counting noses.

• • •

Counting mountain lions roaring
isn't ever very boring.

. . .

Counting rabbits running
rabbit races on the lawn
must be done while one is sunning
and before a rabbit's gone.

. . .

Counting the stars
as they glitter bright white
is lovely indeed
and a marvelous sight
when the air is as fresh
as the first night in fall.
But I always have a feeling
that comes very softly stealing
when my head with stars is reeling
that I didn't count them all.

Over the hills
where the edge of the light
deepens and darkens
to ebony night,
narrow hats high
above yellow bead eyes,
the tatter-haired witches
ride through the skies.

Over the seas
where the flat fishes sleep
wrapped in the slap of the slippery deep,
over the peaks
where the black trees are bare,
where bony birds quiver
they glide through the air.

Silently humming
a horrible tune,
They sweep through the stillness
to sit on the moon.

When dusk is done
and the grey has gone
and the stars blow out
that once were on,
then the pale moon casts
its frozen gleams
and the hollow of night
fills up with dreams:
cats of mice
elves of trolls
cooks of silver spoons and bowls.
Poets dream of rhymes and Rome.
Sailors dream of ships and home.
Princes dream of foreign lands
to conquer
and of ladies' hands.

Dogs dream dreams
of hounds to hares.
The red fox dreams
of grass-green lairs.
While deep in your sleep,
with your dark eyes shut tight,
you dream of the day
that will follow the night.

Wordless words.

A tuneless tune.

Blow out the sun.

Draw down the shade.

Turn off the dog.

Snap on the stars.

Unwrap the moon.

Wish leafy, sleeping trees good night

and listen

to the day shut tight.

"Who are you?"
asked the wind.
"I'm the moon,"
said I.

"And I sit in my spot
near the top of the sky
with a secretive smile
on my elegant face
cold light in my eye
and a pale polished grace.
Glistening
listening
just as I've been
since time was begun.
Watching one star by one
flicker on
flicker out
glowing thin, stouter, stout.
Going stout, thinner, thin
till I'm only a fine
brilliant curve of a line
at the end of your sight
in the deep black of night."

I t's full of the moon
the dogs dance out
through brush and bush and bramble.
They howl and yowl
and growl and prowl.
They amble, ramble, scramble.
They rush through brush.
They push through bush.
They yip and yap and hurr.
They lark around and bark around
with prickles in their fur.
They two-step in the meadow.
They polka on the lawn.
Tonight's the night
the dogs dance out
and chase their tails till dawn.

Where would you be on a night like this

with the wind so dark and howling?

Close to the light

wrapped warm and tight

or there where the cats are prowling?

Where would you wish you on such a night

when the twisting trees are tossed?

Safe in a chair

in the lamp-lit air

or out where the moon is lost?

Where would you be when the white waves roar

on the tumbling storm-torn sea?

Tucked inside

where it's calm and dry

or searching for stars in the furious sky

whipped by the whine of the gale's wild cry

out in the night with me?

This is a song to be sung at night

when nothing is left of you and the light

when the cats don't bark

and the mice don't moo

and the nightmares come and nuzzle you

when there's blackness in the cupboards

and the closet and the hall

and a tipping, tapping, rapping

in the middle of the wall

when the lights have one by one gone out

all over everywhere

and a shadow by the curtains

and a shadow by the chair

bumps a shadow by the chair

then you hide beneath your pillow

with your eyes shut very tight

and you sing

"There's nothing sweeter than

the middle of the night.

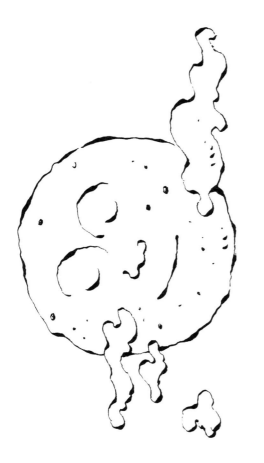

I'm extremely fond of shadows
and I really must confess

that cats and bats don't scare me.
Well, they couldn't scare me less

and most of all I like the things
that slide and slip and creep."

It really is surprising
how fast you fall asleep.

Here we go
bed again
night again

prayers.

Please remember your prayers
fading into the night again
everywhere

here.

There we go
bears.

Count the black-footed bears
resting there on the bed
in the night again.

Here we go
into our lairs.

You have yours
they have theirs
in the woods
where the night rains begin.

Kisses hugs

tucking in

toe to top

sheet to chin.

Lay me down

Earth to Mars

Mom to me.

Lights from cars

wash the wall

brush the moon

drift away

to a song

softly sung in the dark.

It's the song of the stars.

Wake me soon.

Where we are
is very far
from every star.

Dreams are life you live asleep.
But then you wake
and stretch
and yawn
and look around.
The dreams are gone.

Thoughts that were put into words
have been said.
The words were then spoken
and written
and read.
Take a look and go on
we are practically done.

The leftover afternoon light
slips away
on a wind like a sigh.
Watch the day curtains close,
hear the wind going grey
at the edge of the edge
you and I
turn the page
read its message
"The End."

Does the end mean good-bye?

Acknowledgments

I had a cat, 26
If I were a bird, 44
Long ago there was a bear, 94
Spring again, 111
Within a wood, 114
There are reaches of beaches, 137
Thirty thirsty thistles, 154
Under my hood I have a hat, 162

I woke up this morning, 251
Hughbert had a jar of glue, 274
To count myself, 294
Over the hills, 297
When dusk is done, 298
Where would you be on a night
    like this, 303

Uncountable billions, 139
Young Miss Annabella Peach, 140
·Sloping, 142
Flake upon, 167

For wandering walks, 170
When weather's wild and winter
    cold, 188
Sand, 189

I do not understand, 3
Stillness is my secret, 16
If you, 22
One thing that you can say about
    roaring, 29
The night is black, 30
What there is of me to see, 38
My home is a white dome, 43
I am proud, 48
All my legs were very tired, 62
Let me tell you all about me, 74
Come picture this lovely and
    frightening scene, 80
Over a stone, 84
I am a snake, 86
I'm swimming around in the sea, see,
    104

If you stood with your feet in the
    earth, 117
I'm up here, 118
I am softer, 164
When it is dry, 168
I'm scratched and scuffed, 172
It's rotten, 173
I liked growing, 208
My world is an enormous room,
    241
I do not laugh or sing or smile or
    talk, 244
I look like you precisely, 271
When everything has drawn to a
    close, 293
Who are you?, 301

The following poems originally appeared in *Near the Window Tree.* Copyright © 1975 by Karla Kuskin:

I do not wish I were a cat, 11
When a cat is asleep, 12
This cat, 13
Examining the breeze, 14
The terrible cat of black velvet fur, 15
That cat is crazy, 18
Julia loves her Rosalie, 24
Take a word like cat, 31
Tree birds, 39
Buggity, 55
A bug sat in a silver flower, 56
Many people who are smart, 60
Worm, 61
Bugs never speak, 64
Bug, 68
Koala means the world to her, 100
"Cow" sounds heavy, 102

Days that the wind takes over, 156
A tiny house, 174
Where do you get the idea for a poem?, 226
Three wishes, 228
Okay everybody, listen to this, 245
Where have you been, dear?, 246
Running away, 247
The house of snail upon his back, 256
It is grey out, 258
Is six times one a lot of fun, 263
The streets are filled with mustached men, 272
Moon, have you met my mother?, 291
Write about a radish, 292
Wordless words, 300

The following poem originally appeared as *A Boy Had a Mother Who Bought Him a Hat.* Copyright © 1976 by Karla Kuskin:

A boy had a mother who bought him a hat, 178

The following poem originally appeared in *Dogs & Dragons Trees & Dreams.* Copyright © 1980 by Karla Kuskin:

Thoughts that were put into words, 311

The following poem originally appeared as *Night Again.* Copyright © 1981 by Karla Kuskin:

Here we go, 306

Index

A bear went walking, 98

A bird has a nest, 252

A boy had a mother who bought him a hat, 178

A bug sat in a silver flower, 56

A frog's dream, 83

A lot of summer by the sea, 135

A porcupine looks somewhat silly, 101

A snake slipped through the thin green grass, 89

A tiny house, 174

A turtle walks across the lawn, 143

A wizard, 73

All my legs were very tired, 62

Amanda was an alley cat, 17

At the beginning, 144

Being lost, 231

"Bird, 42

Blue bird on a branch, 41

Bug, 68

Buggity, 55

Bugs never speak, 64

Butter, 204

Catherine said, "I think I'll bake, 209

Cats and dogs, 125

Cats take naps, 19

Chocolate, 205

Come picture this lovely and frightening scene, 80

Compare the bears, 99

"Cow" sounds heavy, 102

Days that the wind takes over, 156

Dear shell, 130

Dig deep in you, 232

Do not jump on ancient uncles, 262

Do you hear the parrot squawk?, 50

Don't frown, 134

Dreams are life you live asleep, 310

Ears back, 23

Examining the breeze, 14

Flake upon, 167

For every little blade of grass, 126

For wandering walks, 170

From portal to portal, 88

Good morning, corn, 197

Good-bye toes, 149

Heat, heat, heat, 127

Here we go, 306

Here's a shady glade of lunch trees, 201

Hughbert had a jar of glue, 274

I am a snake, 86
I am beside myself, 238
I am making soup, 206
I am making stew for you, 202
I am proud, 48
I am softer, 164
I am standing on the sand, 286
I am very fond of bugs, 66
I am very fond of you, 239
I am watering the plants, 59
I do not laugh or sing or smile or talk, 244
I do not understand, 3
I do not wish I were a cat, 11
I had a cat, 26
I have a hunch, 207
I have a little guppy, 6
I know a way to open doors, 223
I liked growing, 208
I look like you precisely, 271
I need to read, 221
I said to my mommy, 212
I walk, 65
I will not eat beets, 193
I woke up this morning, 251
I would like to have a pet any kind
    at all, 5
I would like to have a pet any kind
    will do, 107
If I were a bird, 44
If my eyes, 273
If you, 22
If you stood with your feet in the earth,
    117

If you were an onion, 195
I'm scratched and scuffed, 172
I'm shouting, 112
I'm sick of boots, 187
I'm sitting on an old cold star, 254
I'm swimming around in the sea, see, 104
I'm up here, 118
I'm very good at climbing, 260
In August once, 20
In winter there is too much ice, 161
Is six times one a lot of fun?, 263
Isn't it queer, 269
It is grey out, 258
It makes me squirm, 57
It's full of the moon, 302
It's rotten, 173
It's snowing, 169

Julia loves her Rosalie, 24

Koala means the world to her, 100

Leander, Leander, 47
Let me tell you all about me, 74
Liquid isn't solid, 203
Long ago there was a bear, 94
Look out of the window, 151
Look, 76

Many people who are smart, 60
Mice are very fond of it, 196
Mom drinks tea, 198
Moon, have you met my mother?, 291

My bird is small, 36
My head is here, 283
My home is a white dome, 43
My nose is blue, 287
My world is an enormous room, 241

Okay everybody, listen to this, 245
Once there was a cyclops, 242
Once upon, 280
One hundred gulls were standing on the sand, 131
One jay, 37
One raven, 40
One thing that you can say about roaring, 29
Out to walk, 121
Over a stone, 84
Over the hills, 297

People always say to me, 240
Pigeons is a pretty word, 35

Rabbits, 217
Rain lifts my heart, 224
Remember books?, 233
Running away, 247

Sand, 189
(Shortly after six o'clock, 210
Sitting in the sand and the sea comes up, 138
Sloping, 142
Smoke comes out of the dragon's nose, 78

So I picked out a book, 230
Some of us float, 279
Some things you know, 199
Spiders are all right, I guess, 58
Spring again, 111
Stillness is my secret, 16
Summer is gone, 165

Take a word like cat, 31
Take an iguana and bake it, 200
That cat is crazy, 18
The bear coat, 93
The dragon walks, 79
The flower's on the bird, 119
The gulls are not as far as I from you, 51
The house of snail upon his back, 256
The leaves have left without a warning, 157
The lion looks extremely proud, 28
The night is black, 30
The outside me, 278
The running dogs begin to bark, 7
The sky is always in the sky, 265
The sound of a toad, 82
The streets are filled with mustached men, 272
The terrible cat of black velvet fur, 15
The tree has leaves, 175
There are reaches of beaches, 137
There is a bed, 259
There is a fence, 46
There is a me inside of me, 237

There is a tree, 264
There was a hog, 106
There was a man who was so fat, 277
There was a mouse, 25
There was a witch who knitted things,

284

There's a tree by the meadow, 120
These are my knees, 270
Thin or fat, 216
Thirty thirsty thistles, 154
This cat, 13
This is a song to be sung at night, 304
This is my foot, 276
This place began with yellow, green,
    and blue, 132
Thoughts that were put into words,

311

Three wishes, 228
Timothy Tompkins had turnips and tea,

214

To count myself, 294
To eat an egg, 215
Tree birds, 39

Uncountable billions, 139
Under my hood I have a hat, 162
Under the waves the mermaids lounge,

136

We'll play in the snow, 176
What do you do for a living, my dear?,

103

What separates each one of us, 222

What there is of me to see, 38
What would you choose, 248
What's the good of a wagon, 77
When a cat is asleep, 12
When dusk is done, 298
When everything has drawn to a close,

293

When I go walking in the fall, 152
When I went out to see the sun, 155
When it is dry, 168
When the blossoms blossom, 67
When the fields are in flower, 128
When weather's wild and winter cold,

188

When you open your mouth, 166
Where have you been, dear?, 246
Where do you get the idea for a poem?,

226

Where we are, 308
Where would you be on a night like
    this, 303
Whether it's sleeting, 194
Who are you?, 301
Within a wood, 114
Wordless words, 300
Worm, 61
Write about a radish, 292

You are the kind of dog I love, 4
Young Miss Annabella Peach, 140